THE
RIDGE

THE
RIDGE

JOHN RECTOR

THOMAS & MERCER

Published by Thomas & Mercer, Seattle

www.apub.com

Amazon, the Amazon logo, and Thomas & Mercer are trademarks of Amazon.com, Inc., or its affiliates.

ISBN-13: 9781503943933
ISBN-10: 1503943933

Cover design by Faceout Studio

Printed in the United States of America

For Eliot Zane

What is is what must be.

—*Richard Adams,* Watership Down

PART I

1

Then it was Saturday morning.

Megan Stokes stood alone in her living room, cradling a cup of coffee in her hands and staring out the large bay window at the corner house across the street.

The whore was outside again, on her knees in the dirt.

Megan watched her for a while, then she lifted the cup to her lips, blew away the steam, and took a sip.

It burned.

The whore was wearing a floppy white sun hat and over-sized tortoiseshell sunglasses. She had a pair of pink-handled pruning shears in one hand and clippings from her rosebushes in the other, and every few minutes she would sit back on her heels and drop the dead branches into a deep white bucket. Then she'd lean forward, push any loose strands of bottle-black hair from her face, and start cutting again.

Time passed.

Then Tyler came into the room.

He had his blue tie draped loose around his neck and a short stack of manila folders pinned under his arm as he struggled to tighten the lid on his travel mug without spilling the coffee inside.

Megan followed his ghost in the glass as he crossed the room and took his car keys from the bowl by the front door. Then she looked past his reflection to the world outside and ignored him.

"I'm heading to work," he said. "I should be home for dinner. Want me to pick something up?"

Megan didn't say anything.

Tyler stood by the door, waiting. "Megs?"

"I don't care," she said. "Do what you want."

"What's wrong?"

Megan set her coffee cup on the table and nodded toward the window. "She's outside again."

"Who?"

"Rachel Addison."

Tyler crossed the room to where she was standing. When he stepped in behind her and put his hand on her shoulder, Megan had to fight the urge to shrug it away.

"I wish you'd let this go." He angled down, following her gaze. "She's harmless."

"Harmless?" Megan glanced at him over her shoulder. "You're a fool, Tyler."

"Only for you, my love."

Megan felt a twinge of a smile form at the corners of her lips, but she bit down on it, hard, killing it quickly.

Outside, Rachel Addison pushed herself up and brushed the dirt from her jeans with the side of her hand. A young couple jogged by wearing matching yellow-and-blue running outfits. They waved to Rachel as they passed.

Rachel waved back.

"She's biding her time," Megan said. "Women like her always have a plan."

Tyler made a dismissive sound. "And what plan is that? What evil scheme do you think she's hatching over there behind all those roses?"

"Don't do that."

"Don't do what?"

"Don't talk to me like I'm a child," she said. "I'm not a machine, Tyler. I actually have feelings, and I have every right to be pissed about this."

"I think you're overreacting," he said. "She's just friendly, that's all."

"Oh, please." Megan laughed and faced him. "Don't pretend to be so naïve."

"Fine." Tyler set the files on the table next to her coffee cup. "She can be a little more than friendly, but you know I'd never take her up on it. Give me some credit."

Megan looked up at him and tried to think of something else to say. She wanted to argue, to make him see this her way, but she couldn't.

He was right.

Tyler loved her, and she knew he'd never betray her. But that wasn't the point. This wasn't about him, or their marriage, and it wasn't about trust. This was about basic human decency, and it was about boundaries. But most of all, it was about that whore, Rachel Addison, and her complete lack of respect.

And that, Megan couldn't let go.

She turned back to the window and watched Rachel gather her tools and carry them across the yard to the side of the house. She stopped at the garden hose, turned on the water, and rinsed the dirt from her hands. Then she followed the path around to the side of the garage and disappeared behind a wall of lilac bushes.

Once she was out of sight, Megan said, "I'm going over there."

A deep line formed between Tyler's eyebrows. "You're what?"

"I'm going to say something to her."

"You can't do that."

"Watch me." She slid past him and opened the coat closet by the front door. She took out a ratty pair of red Chuck Taylors and slipped them on her bare feet. "It's prison rules out here, Tyler. If someone pushes, you push back."

Tyler didn't say anything, and when she looked up at him, he was smiling.

"What's so funny?"

"This is Willow Ridge, Megs. It's hardly a prison. How

would you know about that kind of thing anyway? You grew up in Lincoln Park."

Megan glared at him. "Don't you have some place to be?"

"I'm not going anywhere until you promise me you won't say anything to her."

"Then get comfortable."

"Come on." His voice was soft, almost pleading. "This isn't worth it."

Megan stepped in front of the mirror by the closet and frowned at her reflection. She ran her hands down the front of her shirt, wiping away a few of the wrinkles.

"If she wants to keep propositioning my husband, and if she doesn't want to take no for an answer, then I've got every right to go over there and—"

"Start a war?"

Megan rolled her eyes. "Don't be so melodramatic."

"That is what you're doing," he said. "We've barely been here three months, and you're already making enemies."

"She started this," Megan said. "It might've been amusing when we first moved here, but I've had enough. And if you don't get why I'm upset, or if you're not on my side, then—"

"I'm always on your side." Tyler stepped closer and took her hands in his. "You know that."

Megan looked up at him. For a moment she felt the anger inside her fade, and she pulled her hands away, fast.

"Then act like it."

Tyler exhaled slowly, and neither of them spoke. The only

sounds in the room were the rolling tick of the grandfather clock in the corner and the steady tapping of her foot on the hardwood floor.

"Rachel Addison is bored and lonely," Tyler said. "She's a sad person, and not someone to get worked up over. Why don't you try to get your mind off of her?"

"And how do I do that?"

"I don't know," he said. "Get out of the house for a while. Find something to do to keep yourself busy."

"I have things to do," Megan said. "I can clean the house, again, or refold the laundry, again." She snapped her fingers. "You know, maybe I'll whip up one of those Jell-O salads with little mandarin oranges and mini-marshmallows floating inside. We'll have it at dinner."

Tyler laughed.

"I wish I was joking."

"A Jell-O salad?"

"Why not? It's practically the 1950s all over again around here. All I need is an A-line dress and some pearls and I'll fit right in."

"Come on, it's not that bad."

"It's not that great, either." She motioned toward the large bay window framing a line of pastel houses across the street. "You've been out there. You know what it's like."

Tyler glanced toward the window, nodded.

"It's a little different here," he said. "I'll give you that, but what do you expect? It's middle-class employee housing. It's going to be a slower life."

"We're hundreds of miles from civilization," Megan said. "A slower life is an understatement."

Tyler checked his watch, frowned. "I can't do this right now. I really have to go."

"Of course you do," she said. "God forbid you're late on a Saturday."

"That's not fair."

Megan held her breath, and when she spoke again, she tried to keep her voice from breaking.

"I had another one of those dreams last night."

"About the girl?"

She nodded. "I almost saw her face this time."

Tyler was quiet for a moment. "We knew it wouldn't be easy here, Megs, but we agreed—"

"I know what we agreed."

He hesitated. "It's a good opportunity here."

"I'm not asking you to quit your job," Megan said. "And I'm not changing my mind about our plans. I just feel like a part of me is missing, and I don't know why. I think maybe I'm—"

"Homesick."

The word hit her hard, and she felt tears press behind her eyes. The last thing she wanted to do was cry in front of him again, so she looked away and bit the insides of her cheeks and waited for the feeling to pass.

Tyler gave her a minute, said, "Are you okay?"

"I'm fine."

"You know we won't be here forever."

Megan nodded and turned toward the window. She ran her fingers under her eyes, silent.

Tyler checked his watch again. Then he stepped closer, put his arms around her shoulders, and pulled her in.

She let herself be pulled.

"I know what you're going to say." She rested her head against his chest, breathing him in. "You need to go."

"That wasn't what I was going to say."

"You want orange Jell-O instead of lime?"

He laughed. "I was going to say we should take some time and go back to Chicago for a few days. I think it'll do us some good."

Megan looked up at him, fast. "Are you being serious?"

"I am."

"Don't tease me about this, Tyler."

He smiled. "I told you they're moving my office at the end of the month. I'm sure I can take two or three days off around then if you want to—"

"But you just started. You don't have vacation time built up. Won't that look bad?"

"I'll tell them I have to clean up a few last-minute things from the move. They'll understand."

"Can you really do that?"

"I really can."

Megan let the idea sink in, and the next time the tears came, she didn't even try to stop them.

"My God," she said. "We could go to Morton's."

"We could see a Cubs game."

"Giant pretzels."

"Smokies."

Megan laughed, and the sound surprised them both. Then she reached up and wiped the tears from her cheeks. Tyler tried to move away, but before he could, she wrapped her arms around his neck and kissed him, long and slow.

When they finally broke, she brushed her lips against his ear and whispered, "How late can you be?"

"Not that late."

"Are you sure?"

He nodded. "But I'll hurry home."

"Yes." She kissed him again. "Do that."

Before he left, Megan helped him tie his tie. Then she watched from the window as he backed down the driveway and out into the street.

She waved as he pulled away, but he didn't notice her.

Once he was out of sight, Megan glanced over at the corner house across the street. Rachel Addison was back outside, watering her rosebushes with the garden hose. She'd changed out of her dirty jeans and into a gold sundress that shone in the sunlight and danced gently over her legs as she moved through the soft summer breeze.

It was a long time before Megan looked away.

2

C hicago.
It was all Megan could think about, and the morning passed by in a blur. She spent most of it lying on the couch, staring up at the ceiling, and dreaming of all the things she wanted to do once they were back home.

The trip couldn't come fast enough.

Eventually, the day began to slip away, so she decided to take Tyler's advice and find something to do. There were still a few boxes left to unpack, and she took care of those first. Then she went upstairs and sorted through the clothes in her closet, laying them out across the bed, and trying to decide what to keep and what to give away.

She had more clothes than she'd ever need, especially living in a place as uneventful as Willow Ridge, but she still couldn't bring herself to part with any of them, and after a while she gave up trying.

Once everything was back in the closet, she walked downstairs and sat on the end of the couch. Her book was lying open on the coffee table. She picked it up and started reading. It was one she'd read before, and she didn't remember thinking much of it the first time, but she wanted to give it another try. Sometimes a second read was all it took, but if not, even a bad book was better than no book.

Megan read for a while, but it didn't take long before her mind began to wander back to Chicago. Eventually, she closed the book and let herself sink into the cushions.

Then she had an idea.

She would surprise Tyler and make dinner.

A small voice in the back of her mind spoke up, reminding her that she couldn't cook, but Megan ignored it.

Things with Tyler had been rough since the move, and she wanted to show him that she cared. A home-cooked meal wasn't much, but it was a good way to say she was sorry.

At least it was a start.

Megan got up and went into the kitchen and checked the pantry. There wasn't a lot to work with, so she took a pen and a notepad from the drawer and started a list.

Her plan was to walk down to the market in the plaza and pick up a couple steaks, some veggies and peppers, and a good bottle of wine.

Maybe even two bottles.

When she finished the list, she sat back and read over it. Everything she needed was there, but it still felt like something was missing. She thought about it, smiled, and then added lime Jell-O, mandarin oranges, and mini-marshmallows.

Tyler would appreciate the joke.

Megan tore the page from the pad and took her purse from the counter and headed for the door.

Outside the sun was bright, and she dug through her purse for her sunglasses. She could hear the low, steady rumble of a lawn mower in the distance, and all around her, the soft green rustle of leaves moving in the warm air.

When she found her sunglasses, she slipped them on and started down the path toward the sidewalk.

The market was a little over a mile away.

She thought about driving, but the rattle in the Corsica's engine had been worse lately, and she didn't want to chance it. She'd had the car since her freshman year in college, and it'd been old when she bought it. The fact it still ran at all was something of a miracle. The truth was, as much as she hated that car, a part of her was going to be sad when it finally died.

Then again, nothing lived forever.

———

The houses in Willow Ridge came in four colors: gray, beige, pale green, and pale blue. Each house had a small porch, a bay window, and a two-car garage. There were no fences allowed, so the yards were divided by rows of tall hedges, smooth cypress trees, and lavender lilac bushes that turned the air heavy and sweet.

THE RIDGE

Megan lived in a gray house, and as she walked along the uncracked sidewalks, past manicured shrubs and emerald lawns, she had to laugh at herself for somehow ending up in the exact kind of place a younger version of herself swore she'd never end up.

Part of her still didn't find it all that funny.

After they'd moved to Willow Ridge, Tyler tried to convince her that she'd eventually get used to it, but she never did. She missed her old neighborhood with its corner markets and constant traffic. She missed the hum of people around her, and the warm, concrete buzz of the city.

Willow Ridge was too impersonal, too sterile.

She felt the change most at the market in the plaza. It was easily the largest market Megan had ever seen; the aisles were always well stocked, and so long that if you stood at one end and looked down toward the other, the perspective became skewed, making it look fake, like you were staring into a painting.

It was unsettling.

There was a smaller store in Ashland, eleven miles north, and for a while Megan had driven there to shop. But they didn't carry much, and the people running the store didn't seem to want her there. They were always polite, always helpful, but she could see the way they looked at her when she came in, and how they watched her when they thought she wasn't paying attention.

Megan tried not to let it bother her.

She understood that Ashland was a small town, and that

she was an outsider, but after a while she grew tired of the stares and the whispers, and eventually she quit going.

That left the market in the plaza.

Once inside, she paced the aisles with the other shoppers, all of them quietly pushing metal carts along polished floors while familiar melodies floated softly in the air overhead. And always, whenever two shoppers passed each other, they would smile and nod, and keep moving.

Megan didn't get it.

When someone passed her in the aisles, she kept her head down and did her best to avoid eye contact.

That seemed easier.

Once she'd found all the items on her list, she made her way to the checkout lanes at the front of the store. The clerk working the register looked like a grad student, attractive in a sullen sort of way, with green eyes and impeccably tousled dark hair.

Megan smiled and handed him a canvas bag.

The clerk stared at it for a moment, and when he finally took the bag, he held it in front of him like it was something dirty.

"I take it you don't see many of those?"

"My first."

Megan held up three fingers. "Always be prepared."

The clerk tilted his head, slightly, like a puppy.

"Boy Scout salute?" She paused. "Forget it."

He did.

Megan kept quiet as he rang up the steaks and the peppers

and the Jell-O. He stopped when he reached the wine, turning the bottle over and reading the label.

"Have you tried that one?" she asked. "I thought it looked good, but who can tell?"

The clerk shook his head.

"My husband and I are celebrating tonight," she said. "We're taking a trip at the end of the month."

She waited for him to respond, but he just slipped the wine into a brown paper sack and set it in the canvas bag. Then he reached for the marshmallows.

"Chicago."

He glanced up.

"It's where we're from," Megan said. "Where I'm from, at least. My husband is from Texas, if you can imagine."

The clerk tapped a button on the register and gave her a price. She paid and watched as he tore the receipt away and handed it to her along with the now-heavy canvas bag.

He smiled. "Come again, ma'am."

Megan's throat tightened.

She started to say something, but instead she shouldered her purse, shifted the bag from one hand to the other, and headed for the door.

She didn't look back.

It was the first time anyone had called her *ma'am* and meant it. She tried telling herself that it didn't matter, but she knew, on some level, it kind of did.

The trip home took longer with the groceries in tow. Part of her regretted not driving, but it was a small part. The day was warm and soft, and as she walked, she could see the Institute at the top of the ridge, the long stretch of buildings bookended by two glass towers rising tall and black against the clear blue sky.

The main building, Tyler's building, was three stories, and fronted by black glass that reflected the sunlight. Tyler had told her once that they could see the entire neighborhood from behind those windows, stretching all the way to the horizon, and that from up there, Willow Ridge looked fake, like a model of a real neighborhood.

Megan tried to imagine that as she walked.

And she thought about Tyler.

She wondered if he was up there now, standing behind those black windows, looking down on this fake model neighborhood, and seeing her.

She liked to think he was.

As she turned the corner onto her street, Megan saw a white Cadillac parked in Rachel Addison's driveway. Rachel was out front, standing next to the car with her arms folded across her chest. Her husband was with her, bent over, digging through the open trunk.

Rachel was saying something to him, and even though she was too far away to hear the exact words, Megan could hear the sharp tone of her voice as she spoke.

Mr. Addison stood back and slammed the trunk shut. Then

he leaned forward, his hands braced on the car, his head low.

Rachel's voice was shrill, unrelenting.

Megan kept her head down and moved fast, hoping they wouldn't notice her, but it didn't work. Mr. Addison saw her, and the expression on his face changed, turned bright. He straightened and lifted one hand into the air.

"Good afternoon, Mrs. Stokes."

Rachel stopped talking, turned, glared at her.

Megan nodded back, silent.

As she passed, she noticed a slow smirk slide across Rachel's lips, and for an instant, something primal flashed deep inside her.

She's laughing at me.

Megan felt a sudden, violent rush of anger. It was so strong that for a moment she had to fight the urge to drop her bags and run across the street with her fists clenched.

Then she thought of Tyler, and the urge faded.

She kept walking.

When she got home, she locked the door behind her and carried the groceries into the kitchen. She set the bags on the counter and closed her eyes.

The anger was still there, simmering just under the surface.

She reminded herself that in a few weeks she'd be back home in Chicago, far away from Rachel Addison and the endless, soul-killing monotony of Willow Ridge.

It took a while, but eventually it helped.

3

I t was almost six o'clock.

The table was set, the candles were lit, and the grill on the stove was hot. The steaks were seasoned and ready to go, and Megan had just started to cut the peppers when the phone rang.

"Hey, Megs."

Tyler's voice had a tired tone to it, and Megan could tell right away that something was wrong. She wiped the blade of the knife clean with a dish towel and slid it back into the block beside the stove. Then she leaned against the counter and waited.

"It looks like I'm going to be here for a while," Tyler said. "I'm really sorry."

"What happened?"

"There's a problem in the lab. It's a long story, but they asked me to stick around."

"What kind of problem?"

"You want the details?"

"No, I guess not." She reached out and turned the heat down on the grill. "It's just disappointing. I had a surprise waiting for you."

"Don't remind me. It's been on my mind all day."

Megan smiled. "Not that surprise."

"Really? Now I'm intrigued."

"I made dinner tonight."

Tyler paused. "You cooked?"

"That's right."

"Like an actual meal?"

"Don't sound so shocked," she said. "I've got candles on the table and a bottle of wine ready to go, too."

"Save the wine until I get home. I have a feeling I'm going to need it."

"That bad?"

Tyler started to explain, but he stopped himself. "It doesn't matter. I'm sorry I ruined your surprise."

"I'll keep everything warm for you."

He made a soft sound. "Everything?"

The hint in his voice was more than obvious, and Megan smiled. "Why not? It's a special occasion, after all."

"Yeah? What's the occasion?"

"Our trip," she said. "I know, it's dumb, but I want to celebrate. I've been thinking about it all day."

Tyler was quiet.

The silence dragged on for too long, and a cold spot formed in the pit of her stomach.

"What's wrong?"

"Nothing," Tyler said. "Let me wrap up here, and I'll head home as soon as I can, okay?"

The tone of his voice had changed, and Megan didn't like it. All at once her legs felt heavy. She pulled a chair away from the table and sat down.

"What happened?" she asked.

"What do you mean?"

She let the silence hang between them, and she closed her eyes.

"We're not going are we?"

"I never said that."

"You told me that weekend would work—" Her voice cracked. "You said you could take the time off."

"Can we talk when I get home?" he asked. "I can explain everything then."

"Tell me what happened."

"Nothing happened." Tyler's voice was barely above a whisper. "They changed the schedule, and now they need me here that weekend. I don't know what it's about, and they didn't go into specifics."

"But your office? They're moving your office."

"Apparently that doesn't matter."

Megan wanted to say something else, but she didn't know what, and she was afraid if she opened her mouth she would start to cry. So instead, she grabbed the wine bottle off the table and reached for the corkscrew.

"We'll talk when I get home," Tyler said. "I'm not in the most private place right now."

Megan pulled the cork on the bottle, then picked up one of the wineglasses and filled it.

"Megan?"

"Fine," she said. "We'll talk when you get home."

Tyler hesitated. "This doesn't mean we can't go at all. We'll have other chances."

She lifted the wineglass and took a long drink, feeling it burn all the way down.

"Are you there?"

"I'll see you when you get home," she said. "I need to finish cooking dinner."

"Okay." He paused. "Megs, I'm really sorry."

Megan hung up and dropped the phone on the table.

She stayed there for a long time, emptying and refilling her wineglass while the relentless pulse of the grandfather clock ticked softly away in the next room.

———

She burned the steaks, but it didn't matter.

After finishing the first bottle of wine, Megan pulled the cork on the second. She started to refill her glass, but then she changed her mind. The air in the house was thick with smoke and the smell of burnt meat. She could taste it in the back of her throat, making it hard to breathe, so she got up and grabbed the bottle and carried it outside and sat on the porch steps.

The neighborhood was quiet.

The evening sun was leaning toward the west, and the moon was rising in the blue east. It hung there, weightless and thin, a pale sliver in a slowly darkening sky.

She lifted the bottle to her lips and drank.

"Good evening, Mrs. Stokes."

Megan glanced over at the house next door and saw Edna Davidson standing in her front yard. She had one end of a rope leash in her hand, and she was struggling to wrap a yellow chiffon scarf over her hair. At the other end of the leash was the oldest brown poodle Megan had ever seen.

His name was Mr. Jitters.

"Hi, Mrs. Davidson," Megan said. "Off for a walk?"

"Hope to be," she said, still struggling with the scarf. "If I can get myself situated."

"Would you like some help?"

"Oh, I think I can manage."

Megan took another drink and watched the battle.

Once Mrs. Davidson had the scarf in place, she bent down and whispered something to Mr. Jitters. Then she looked up at Megan and smiled. "You have a good night."

Megan held up the bottle. "I plan to."

Mrs. Davidson's smile faded. She turned back to Mr. Jitters, lying on the grass. "Come on, time to go."

Mr. Jitters didn't move, so she pulled him along, gently at first, then harder. The dog whined as she dragged him across the grass toward the sidewalk, but eventually he gave in. The gears clicked into place, and his small legs moved in a quick brown blur beneath him.

Megan watched them go. Then she set the bottle on the steps between her feet and leaned back, resting her weight on her hands. *Soon,* she thought, *the sun will go down, and the lights along the street will come on. The windows in the houses will glow bright, and the entire neighborhood will burn into evening.*

It was the same thing every single night.

She thought about that for a while, trying to picture what her life in Willow Ridge would be like five years down the road, ten years, twenty years.

For all she knew, she would be living in Willow Ridge for the rest of her life. Sure, it was possible they'd move back to Chicago someday, but what if they didn't?

What if this was their last stop?

In a few decades, she could be the one wearing a chiffon scarf over her hair and dragging a half-dead dog along the sidewalk.

The mental image made her laugh, and she reached for the bottle and took a drink. She'd long since stopped tasting the wine, and she knew from experience that that wasn't a good sign, but she didn't care.

Tonight she was taking a break from caring.

Megan started to take another drink, but then she heard

laughter to her right and lowered the bottle. Mrs. Davidson was standing on the corner across the street. She was talking to Rachel Addison while Mr. Jitters sniffed at the grass by her feet. From where Megan sat, it looked like Rachel was doing all the talking.

Once again, she got a flash of her future.

She saw herself, fifteen years on, living in the same gray house with a husband she rarely saw, surrounded by unchallenging people in a cookie-cutter neighborhood. Maybe she'd be less like Edna Davidson with old Mr. Jitters, and more like Rachel Addison, growing rainbows of roses in her garden, and desperately trying to seduce other women's husbands.

In a few years, maybe *she'd* be the neighborhood whore.

This time, Megan didn't laugh.

Down the street, she watched Rachel whisper something to Mrs. Davidson, then reach out and touch her arm before throwing her head back, cackling at the sky.

Megan heard the sound in her bones.

When the conversation ended, Mrs. Davidson continued down the sidewalk, dragging Mr. Jitters behind her. Megan watched until she turned the corner.

Then she looked back at Rachel.

She was standing at the edge of her yard, stacking planter pots, one inside the other. When she finished, she picked them up and carried them around to the far side of her garage.

Megan lifted the bottle and drank, grinding her teeth.

When Rachel didn't come back outside, Megan stood and corked the bottle. She left it sitting on the porch steps as she crossed the yard and walked into the street.

Behind her, the setting sun burned red and the evening shadows stretched long and dark toward Rachel's house.

Megan didn't know what she was going to say to her when she saw her, but she didn't think it mattered.

She knew how the conversation would go.

4

There were two ceramic turtles on the porch, one on either side of the door. Their shells were polished, dark and smooth, and painted a deep green. Megan stared at them for a moment, then wiped the bottom of her shoe on one before reaching out and ringing the doorbell.

No one answered.

She glanced over her shoulder at her house, and for the first time she wondered if she was making the right decision. The answer seemed obvious, but she rang the doorbell again anyway.

This time when no one answered, she reached out and knocked. Then she heard a voice coming from far off to her right.

"I'm in the garage."

Megan turned from the door and started down the steps. Her foot missed the last one, and she stumbled forward. For a second, she thought she was going to fall face-first into the grass, but she caught herself before she went down. She straightened up and looked around to see if anyone had noticed, but the streets were quiet.

She was alone.

Megan's heart was beating hard, and she could taste the peppery combination of warm wine and stomach acid in the back of her throat. She tried to swallow it away, but it didn't help.

She took a deep breath, then followed the path around the house to the garage. The large overhead door was closed, but the side door was partly open, and a pale fluorescent light leaked out onto a thin cement path and a line of square hedges.

There was movement inside the garage, and when Megan stepped through the door she saw Rachel Addison in her gold sundress, standing on a wooden ladder next to a long metal workbench. She was stacking red clay pots on the top of a tall row of shelves that ran along the back wall from one end of the garage to the other. The shelf to Megan's right was lined with ceramic lawn gnomes and several coiled garden hoses.

Everything was perfectly organized.

Rachel had her back to the door, and when she didn't turn, Megan coughed, loud.

Rachel jumped at the sound, and the ladder wobbled under her. She reached out and grabbed the shelves for balance. One of the clay pots slipped out of her hand and fell, shattering on the cement floor.

Rachel looked back at Megan, standing in the doorway.

"You scared the shit out of me."

Megan started to apologize, more out of habit than actual regret, but then she remembered why she was there, and she didn't say a word.

Rachel climbed down the ladder and stood over the broken pot, frowning.

"These aren't cheap, you know."

When Megan didn't say anything, Rachel shook her head then bent down and began picking up the bigger shards and dropping them into a metal bin. She took a plastic dustpan and hand broom from one of the shelves under the workbench and swept the smaller pieces into a pile.

Megan watched her work, ignoring the sour taste of wine in her throat and the way the room gently swayed around her.

"Am I supposed to guess why you're here, or are you planning on telling me?" Rachel asked.

"You know who I am?"

"Of course I know who you are."

Megan swallowed hard, hoping her voice wouldn't crack. "I thought you might only know my husband."

Rachel stopped sweeping, and Megan saw a thin smile form on her lips as she lifted the dustpan and tapped it empty against the inside of the metal bin.

"How is Tyler?"

Tyler.

Megan's cheeks burned red. She started to say something

she knew she shouldn't, but she stopped herself before the words were out. When she did speak, she kept her voice even and calm.

"Mrs. Addison, I think you and I need to clear a few things up."

"Do we?" Rachel slid the broom and dustpan back onto the shelf under the workbench and straightened, brushing the dirt from her hands. "Well, I'm always in favor of clarity. You don't mind if I work while we talk, do you?"

Her voice was pure sugar.

"I know what you've been doing," Megan said. "I know what you've been saying to him."

"To whom?"

"To Tyler." She paused, added, "My husband."

Rachel laughed, then bent down and picked up three of the red clay pots, stacking them one inside the other. "You're going to have to refresh my memory. I say a lot of things to a lot of people."

Megan felt a slight tremble in her legs as she watched Rachel climb the ladder. She wasn't nervous, not anymore, but her chest ached, and the wine was making it hard to keep her thoughts straight.

She squeezed her hands into fists, forcing herself to focus, and stepped closer.

"He won't do it, you know."

"Won't do what?"

"Take you up on your offer."

"My offer?" Rachel pushed the pots into place on the top shelf and climbed down. "What offer is that?"

The anger inside her turned sour. Megan tried to laugh it away, but the sound came out forced and unnatural, even to her.

"Is that really how you want to do this?"

Rachel frowned and reached for another stack of pots. "I'm sorry, but I'm not sure what it is we're doing."

"You're making a fool out of yourself," Megan said. "You're chasing a married man, and you—"

"I'm what?"

"Don't deny it," she said. "Just don't."

Rachel set the pots back on the floor and stepped closer. "I think you've made a mistake."

"Tyler didn't want me to come here," Megan said. "And I almost didn't. I was going to let it go, like always. But then I thought about you and your goddamn rosebushes and this shitty neighborhood and—"

"Megan."

"I was even nervous walking over here." She laughed. "Not now, though. Now I just feel sorry for you."

Rachel stared at her, unblinking.

Megan stared back.

After a moment, it occurred to her that there was nothing left for her to say. She'd done what she came to do. She'd made her point, told her what she thought of her, and now she could leave, satisfied.

But then Rachel spoke.

"How old are you, Megan?"

The question stopped her. "Excuse me?"

"Until today, I've only seen you from a distance." Rachel stepped forward, studying her face. "You look quite a bit younger up close. What are you, twenty-four? Twenty-five?"

"Twenty-seven."

Rachel repeated the number under her breath.

"What does my age have to do with anything?"

"Nothing and everything." She turned back to the pots, lifted one of the stacks, and started up the ladder again. "You're an attractive young woman, Megan. Most of that is due to your age, of course, but not all of it. You're very lucky."

"Mrs. Addison, if you think I—"

"Call me Rachel."

Megan stopped talking. She moved her hands behind her back and squeezed them into fists, digging her fingernails into her skin, grounding herself in the pain.

She knew what Rachel was trying to do.

The compliments, the familiarity.

Rachel was trying to defuse the situation, but it wasn't going to work. She wasn't going to forget why she was there, and she wasn't going to back down.

"Mrs. Addison, I don't think you understand why I'm here."

"I know exactly why you're here, Mrs. Stokes," she said, emphasizing the name. "You're here because you feel threatened."

Megan smiled, silent.

"Oh, not by me." Rachel climbed down and picked up the last stack of pots. "You feel threatened by your husband."

"That's ridiculous."

"Is it?" She adjusted the pots in her arm and started back up the ladder. "I believe, if you truly trusted your husband, you wouldn't have felt the need to storm over here, and we wouldn't be having this conversation."

"I trust Tyler completely."

"He only has eyes for you, is that right?"

"Are you saying he doesn't?"

"I'm saying most young wives feel that way about their husbands, and most come to realize that it's rarely true."

"You don't know what you're talking about."

"Maybe not." Rachel shrugged. "But I do know that if you show me the most beautiful woman in the world, I'll show you the man who's sick of fucking her."

The muscles in Megan's jaw went slack.

Rachel laughed.

"Oh, don't look so shocked," she said. "You're not a child, Megan, and I'm not telling you anything you didn't already have figured out ten years ago. Men are who they are, and some things never change."

Rachel stared down at her, waiting for her to respond, but Megan had no words. All she could think about was running across the garage and pulling her off that ladder and wrapping her hands around her throat and . . .

Squeezing.

But she didn't.

Instead, she walked away.

She was almost out the door when Rachel called after her. "I hope you feel we've cleared things up, Megan. Do me a favor and close the door on your way out."

Megan stopped walking.

Her chest was tight, and she could hear her pulse pounding behind her ears. She turned and watched Rachel rearranging the lines of red clay pots along the top shelf.

Ignoring her.

I'm being dismissed.

The thought dug in deep, rotting inside her. She could feel her anger building to a scream, but the scream never came. Instead, a cold, calming wave passed over her, and all the rage and frustration faded into nothing.

Rachel glanced over her shoulder.

"Was there something else?"

Megan turned to the shelf next to her, staring at the rows of ceramic lawn gnomes. She reached for the first one in line, picked it up, and turned it over in her hands. Then she tossed it, high into the air, and watched it fall.

It hit the cement and cracked at her feet.

Rachel gasped. "What are you doing?"

Megan smiled up at her, then reached for another gnome. This time, she threw it hard against the wall to her left.

The sound it made when it broke was delicious.

"Are you out of your mind?" Rachel hurried and pushed the last of the pots into place on the shelf. "Get out. Get the hell out of here, now."

Megan picked up another gnome.

This one had a long, flat nose, and a tiny crooked hat. Megan thought it was adorable, and she held it up for Rachel to see.

Rachel froze on the ladder, pointed.

"Give it to me."

"This one?" She held it out. "You want this one?"

Megan didn't wait for an answer. Instead, she stepped forward and threw the gnome as hard as she could.

Her aim was off, and it missed high, shattering against the wall above Rachel's head.

Rachel ducked, covering herself with one arm as a scatter of tiny ceramic pieces dropped around her.

When she looked up, there was fury in her eyes.

"You crazy bitch."

Megan reached for another gnome.

"No!"

Rachel started down, moving fast. She'd only taken one step when the ladder shifted, and her foot slipped between the rungs.

For an instant, time seemed to stop.

Megan watched Rachel's hands come away from the rails, and she heard her make a small, panicked sound as her arms pinwheeled desperately in the air.

Then she fell.

Halfway down, Rachel's head struck the edge of the work-bench. There was a loud crack, like the splitting of dry wood, and then silence.

Megan lifted her hands, covering her mouth.

Every muscle in her body locked.

She could see Rachel lying on the ground by the work-bench, her gold sundress up around her waist, her legs twitching on the cold cement floor.

Megan moved closer, forcing each step.

Rachel was on her back, her hair covering her face. One arm was pinned beneath her, the other out to the side, finger-nails clawing at the dirty floor.

Megan knelt and brushed the hair from Rachel's face. Then, when she saw the unnatural way her neck was bent, all the air rushed out of her lungs, and she pulled back.

"Oh my God."

Rachel's eyes were open, darting from side to side, un-focused, panicked. Her breath was shallow, and her mouth opened and closed, but made no sound.

"Don't move," Megan said, feeling tears on her cheeks. "I'm going to call for help."

She started to get up, but then Rachel's eyes focused on her, and she stopped.

A thin line of saliva ran from the corner of Rachel's mouth and pooled on the floor beneath her head. Then she spoke, her voice wet and broken.

"I can't breathe . . . I can't breathe . . . I can't breathe . . ."

Rachel repeated the words, over and over, her voice hitching and growing thinner each time.

"You're going to be fine," Megan said. "Just don't move."

Rachel's body shuddered.

Megan didn't know what to do.

She put her hands on Rachel's shoulders and tried to hold her still. Then Rachel made a hard, choking sound deep in her throat, and white foam bubbled out over her lips.

"Oh God. No, no, no," Megan said, crying. "Please, please don't."

Rachel's body vibrated under her, and the choking grew louder. Megan kept her hands on Rachel's shoulders, but she couldn't help her, and she knew it. All she could do was watch as the light slowly faded from her eyes.

Then the shaking stopped, and she was alone.

5

Megan ran out of Rachel's garage and up the street toward her house. There were tears on her face, and a sharp, glowing pain in the center of her head. She tried to block it, but it grew brighter with each step, and by the time she'd reached her house, the pain was blinding.

She stopped at the bottom of the porch steps and closed her eyes. She tried pressing her fingertips against the sides of her head, but the pain didn't fade.

When she opened her eyes, she saw the corked wine bottle on the step where she'd left it. She grabbed it on her way up, then stopped outside the front door.

She heard voices coming from up the street.

Edna Davidson was walking along the sidewalk. She was carrying Mr. Jitters in the crook of her arm, and she wasn't alone. Another woman was with her. She was younger than Edna, and she wore a white shirt and jeans.

Megan didn't recognize her.

When they saw her, they waved.

Megan waved back. Then she stepped inside, locked the bolt behind her, and leaned against the closed door.

The pain in her head was screaming.

She closed her eyes again and took a deep breath, counting a slow, easy rhythm. The repetition helped, and for a brief moment, the pain faded and her head cleared.

Then she saw her again.

Rachel Addison, lying bent on the garage floor, her fingernails scraping against the cement, her neck . . .

I can't breathe . . .

Megan pushed away from the door, trying to shake the image from her mind, then ran down the hallway toward the kitchen. She set the wine bottle on the counter and reached for the phone.

Her fingers hung over the keypad, but she didn't dial.

Who was she supposed to call?

Her first thought was to call an ambulance, but that didn't seem right. Rachel Addison was dead. Paramedics wouldn't be able to help. Besides, seeing an ambulance in front of her house would only bring out the neighbors.

The neighbors.

Megan felt a new jolt of panic.

Once the neighbors found out, they would all gather along the street in hungry packs, whispering and gossiping. And since she was the last person to see Rachel alive, it wouldn't take long before their attention shifted to her.

And then the questions would start.

But you did kill her. It is your fault.

Megan pressed her fingers against the spot between her eyes and tried to force that voice away.

Instead, it grew louder.

What are you going to tell the police?

The thought filled her.

For the first time, Megan saw exactly how the situation was going to unfold. She was going to be blamed for Rachel Addison's death, and there was nothing she could do to stop it.

The realization trembled through her.

Even if she explained everything, told the police that Rachel lost her balance and fell, that it had been an accident, it wouldn't matter.

They would still blame her.

They would want to know why she was there, and why there were broken ceramic figures on the ground. They would ask why it looked like there had been a fight, and Megan wouldn't have an answer.

She could tell them she stopped by to visit, like any good neighbor. Except, she wasn't a good neighbor. She had never stopped by to visit anyone in Willow Ridge, and it wouldn't take long before someone pointed that out.

And then the rumors would start.

Megan shut her eyes and tried to think, but her thoughts spun away with the wine. Eventually, she hung up the phone and leaned against the counter.

Her stomach cramped.

A flood of warm wine and stomach acid crawled up into the back of her throat, and she ran across the kitchen to the sink, leaning over just in time.

She thought it would never stop, but it did.

Megan turned on the water and rinsed the sink. Then she cupped her hands under the faucet and took a long drink, swishing the cold water in her mouth, spitting into the drain.

She felt better.

Once again, she went over everything that'd happened, and this time it was easier for her to see it as an accident and not her fault.

Rachel Addison lost her balance and fell.

That was the truth.

Megan went back to the counter, feeling steadier, and picked up the phone. She was about to dial the number for an ambulance when the doorbell rang.

She stopped, listened.

Her hand, frozen over the keypad, began to shake.

A minute passed. There was a click on the line, and a familiar robotic female voice said, "If you'd like to make a call, please hang up and—"

The doorbell rang again.

Megan inhaled deep, closed her eyes, and let the air out slowly. Then she set the phone back in the cradle and started toward the door.

The woman outside was halfway to the sidewalk when Megan opened the door and stepped out. When she saw her, the woman stopped and turned back, smiling.

"I thought I saw you go inside," the woman said. "I hope this isn't a bad time."

She was wearing faded jeans and a white shirt with the sleeves rolled up to the elbows. She had a wooden clipboard in her hand, held close to her chest. It took a minute before Megan recognized her.

She was the woman walking with Edna Davidson, the one who'd waved.

"I can come back another time if you'd like."

Megan glanced past her toward Rachel's house, silent.

"Is everything okay?" the woman asked.

All at once Megan realized she was acting strange, and that she needed to pull herself together.

"No, it's—" She shook her head. "It's fine."

"Are you sure? You never know just dropping by like this." The woman came closer, held out her hand. "Fiona Matheson. I live a few blocks down."

"Megan Stokes."

They shook, and Fiona held Megan's hand as she spoke.

"I've been meaning to come by and introduce myself for a while. I try to meet all the new neighbors. I'm usually pretty good about it, but lately it's been one thing after another. I'm sure you know how it goes."

"I do," Megan said. "It's life."

"Exactly." Fiona smiled, let go of her hand. "It's life."

There was a pause, and for a moment neither of them said anything. Then Fiona motioned toward Rachel's house on the corner. "I saw you leaving the Addison place, so I thought I'd stop by on my way over and say hello."

"Your way over?"

"To see Rachel." She held up the clipboard. "I've put it off for as long as I can. I figured now or never."

"You're going to talk to Rachel?"

"My next stop."

Megan's stomach dropped, and she leaned against the doorframe. For a second she thought she was going to be sick again. Then the feeling passed.

"Are you sure you're okay?" Fiona stepped closer. "You look like a bleached sheet."

"A little light-headed," Megan said. "But I'm fine."

"Why don't I come back another time. I didn't mean—"

"No." Her voice came out louder than she intended, and Fiona's eyes went wide. Megan laughed, trying to cover, and said, "It's fine, really. It'll pass."

Fiona watched her, and Megan could tell she was trying to read her.

"Well, that's good to hear," Fiona said. "But I should probably go anyway. I need to see Rachel before it gets too late."

A rush of panic broke inside of her, and Megan tried to think of something she could say to make her stay, or at least stall her.

She pointed to the clipboard. "Something important?"

Fiona looked down at the clipboard as if seeing it for the first time, and shook her head. "More of a tradition around here than anything. I'm signing up volunteers for the Ashland Renovation Project. We do it twice a year."

"What kind of renovations?"

"Infrastructure stuff, mostly," she said. "We help with cleanup and repairs. A few minor improvements, that kind of thing."

"Like fixing the broken streetlight?"

Fiona's eyes sparkled. "You noticed that?"

"I thought I was the only one who did."

"It might just be the two of us." She raised a finger and made a wide circling motion in the air as she spoke. "Most people here don't go to Ashland if they can avoid it. They're not always the friendliest bunch down there."

"Yeah," Megan said. "I've noticed."

There was another long silence, and it took all her self-control to keep from looking over at Rachel's house.

"Speaking of unfriendly people." Fiona held up the clipboard. "I've been putting Rachel off long enough, but I'll make sure to stop by another time so we can talk. I hope you feel better."

Megan opened her mouth, desperate to say something to keep Fiona from leaving, but there were no words.

Fiona turned and walked away; she was almost to the sidewalk when Megan finally found her voice.

"Would you like a glass of wine?"

Fiona stopped and turned around. "I'm sorry?"

"Wine." Megan thumbed back toward the door. "I just opened a bottle if you'd like to join me."

"Normally, you wouldn't have to ask twice," she said. "But are you sure you're feeling up to it?"

Megan wasn't sure, but she also didn't see any other option. If Fiona discovered Rachel's body before she'd had a chance to report what'd happened, her role in Rachel's death would go from questionable to suspicious in a hurry.

"I think a drink might be exactly what I need." Megan nodded toward Rachel's house. "Can you put Mrs. Addison off for another night?"

Fiona stared at her, and for one terrible moment Megan was sure she was going to say no. If that happened, she didn't know what she was going to do.

But then Fiona smiled.

"You," she said, "are going to be a bad influence on me, I can tell."

Megan shrugged. "There are worse things to be."

Fiona laughed and climbed the porch steps.

6

Megan poured the wine and tried not to think about Rachel as Fiona wandered down the hallway, examining the photographs hung along the wall.

She stopped at one and said, "This is a nice picture."

"Our first anniversary," Megan said, handing her a glass. "Almost seven years ago. We went to this little Italian restaurant by our old apartment in Chicago. Tiny place with checkered tablecloths, candles in Chianti bottles, totally cliché."

"Sounds romantic."

Megan nodded. "It was."

Fiona sipped her wine. "How are you two adjusting to Stepford?"

"Stepford?"

Fiona laughed and waved the comment away. "It's an old joke around here, but it fits. Don't tell me you haven't noticed."

"I've noticed," Megan said. "I just didn't think anyone else saw it. Everyone here seems so—"

"Oblivious?"

"I was going to say *content.*"

Fiona took another drink and turned back to the photos on the wall. "Same thing, if you ask me."

Megan kept quiet and watched as Fiona worked her way down the hallway, passing by some of the photos, smiling at others until she reached the end.

"You two make a cute couple."

"Thank you."

"I'm not just saying that, either. You two fit together. You must've been made from the same mold."

"Are you married?"

"Married?" She shook her head. "Wasn't in the stars for me, and I'm fine with that. I'm better on my own."

"I never thought I'd get married."

"Yet you did."

"And no one was more surprised than me."

Fiona stared at her, and Megan realized she was waiting for her to go on. But she didn't know what else to say, so she changed the subject. "How did you wind up here?"

"In Stepford?"

Megan smiled. "Yeah, in Stepford."

"I work on the ridge, just like everyone else."

"You're at the Institute?"

Fiona nodded, sipped her wine.

"What do you do?"

"Administrative work," she said. "It's mostly organization and delegation. It's not as demanding as what the engineers and technicians do every day, so that gives me more time to do other things."

"Like the Ashland project."

"Exciting, isn't it?"

"My husband works at the Institute," Megan said. "He's a technician. We don't see much of each other these days. They keep him pretty busy."

"I wish I could tell you it gets easier," Fiona said. "Do you know what he's working on?"

Megan shook her head. "He's tried to explain it to me, but that stuff makes my eyes gloss over. He's the math and science half of our marriage, while I'm—"

"The artist."

Megan looked up and saw a hint of a smile on Fiona's lips. It occurred to her that this woman knew more about her than she was letting on, or at least she thought she did.

"I wouldn't go that far."

"Really?" Fiona's smile faded, replaced with genuine surprise. "Because I was just talking to Edna Davidson before I came over here, and she told me you were something of a big deal back in Chicago."

"She was exaggerating."

"What did she tell me?" Fiona cocked her head, as if trying to recall the memory. "One of Chicago's most promising

49

young artists. She said you made some magazine's thirty-under-thirty list, and that you were up for a rather prestigious award, or maybe it was a grant. Is that true?"

"It's true that I didn't get it." Megan lifted the glass, touched the wine to her lips, but didn't drink. "I haven't worked in months."

"Why is that?"

"I guess I needed a break," Megan said. "Then Tyler was transferred out here to the Institute, and we moved."

"But you'll go back to it, won't you?"

"Haven't yet," she said. "Tyler's been good about not pushing, but I think that's because he's worried about me starting it up again. When I'm working, it can be tough on both of us."

"How so?"

The bluntness of the question surprised her.

Megan paused, trying to decide if she wanted to talk about it. The problem was that she didn't think about those days very often, and when she did, all she could remember was a deep gray emptiness, and a heavy, weighted feeling of being broken.

Also, Fiona was a complete stranger.

Except, she didn't feel like a stranger.

There was something comforting about her, something almost familiar. Whatever it was, it immediately put Megan at ease and made her want to talk.

"I lost the joy in it," she said. "My mother had just died

unexpectedly, and after that, whenever I sat down to work, the walls would start to close in. Tyler always took the brunt of it."

"So you moved here?"

"It seemed like a good place to begin again."

Fiona laughed. "Well, you're right about that."

Eventually, they made their way into the dining room and sat at the table. Outside, the sun had gone down, and the windows were empty and black. Megan's mind flashed to Rachel lying in her garage, and she wondered how long it would be before someone discovered her body.

She forced the thought away, and this time when she lifted her glass, she drank.

They talked for the next hour. Fiona asked Megan about Tyler and about their life in Chicago, and once Megan got started, she didn't hold back.

It'd been so long.

When Megan finished, Fiona divided the last of the wine between their glasses and told her she was impressed with how much she remembered about those days.

Megan started to ask her what she meant, but then Fiona looked at her watch and said, "Oh, it's late. I should go."

And the world came rushing back.

"Already?" Megan said, trying to keep her voice steady. "I might have another bottle back there somewhere."

Fiona shook her head, then lifted her glass and emptied it in two swallows. "Ask me another night." She pushed away from the table and stood up. "This was fun. I'd love to do it again."

Megan told her she would, too, and it was the truth. Then she asked, "Are you still going to see Rachel tonight?"

Fiona shook her head. "I'll try and stop by tomorrow, unless something else comes up and I can put it off again." She crossed her fingers, faking a prayer.

"You two don't get along?"

Fiona's eyes went wide. "Oh hell. I'm sorry, are you two friends? Typical me, talk first, think later."

"No," Megan said, smiling. "We're not friends."

"See," Fiona said, snapping her fingers. "You do have something in common with everyone else around here."

"Is she that bad?"

"Let's just say she's a challenge."

"Then why try to recruit her?"

"Because she's our resident horticulturist. Haven't you noticed?"

"I've seen her roses."

"Those are just her hobby. She does all the landscape design for the community, all the public areas, even the Central Plaza. It would make things easier for us if she'd agree to help in Ashland, but she won't."

"It sounds like she's busy."

"There are labor teams that do most of the actual work." Fiona hesitated, then whispered, "Rachel's just a bitch."

They both laughed.

It didn't seem right, considering what she knew, but Megan was surprised at how little it bothered her.

She walked Fiona to the door and stood on the porch. The air outside was cool and fresh, and the clear night sky was an explosion of stars.

"Tell Tyler I look forward to meeting him next time."

"I will."

Megan watched her walk away, and when Fiona reached the sidewalk, she turned and waved over her shoulder.

Megan waved back.

Once Fiona was gone, she looked toward Rachel's house on the corner. There were no lights on, and the house stood silent and dark.

Inside, the grandfather clock began to chime.

Megan tried to decide what to do next, but there were no good options. Her head was heavy, and her thoughts were thick with wine, but by the time the chiming stopped, she thought she had an answer.

She went back inside and down the hall toward the kitchen. She picked up the phone and stared at the keypad, listening to the low drone of the dial tone. Then she took a deep breath and began to dial.

Tyler answered on the third ring.

7

M egan turned off the lights in the living room and stood at the front window with her arms folded over her chest, waiting for Tyler.

She didn't tell him what'd happened when she called, only that he needed to come home, that it was an emergency. He'd pushed her, trying to get her to explain, but she didn't want to tell him anything over the phone.

She wanted to see him face-to-face.

Outside, the streetlights glowed pale over the sidewalks, and the windows of the other houses shone gold behind long rows of hedges. Occasionally, a car would drive by, and each time it did, Megan's chest would tighten, and her breath would catch in her throat.

But the cars never stopped.

Eventually, she saw a familiar set of headlights turn on the street and pull into the driveway.

Tyler was home.

She backed away from the window and took a deep breath, trying to calm her frayed nerves. She heard his car door shut, and her stomach twisted as she realized she had no idea what she was going to say to him.

Then the door opened, and Tyler came inside.

"Megan?"

His voice was urgent, tense.

He turned on the light, and when he saw her standing there, he jumped back, startled.

"Megan, what the hell?" He came closer, reaching out, grabbing her shoulders. "Are you okay? What happened?"

"I—" The words stuck in her throat. "There—there was an accident."

Tyler asked her again if she was okay, and when she told him she was fine, some of the tension seemed to fade. His grip on her shoulders loosened, and several new questions appeared behind his eyes.

"What happened?"

Megan looked up at him and a tear ran down her cheek. She wiped it away with the back of her hand.

Tyler led her to the couch, and they both sat, facing each other. He took her hands, pressing them between his.

He told her to start at the beginning.

So she did.

———

"Are you sure?" Tyler was up, pacing back and forth through the living room. "You're positive that she's—"

"Yes," Megan said. "I saw it happen. I watched her—"

"Oh my God." He stopped at the window and ran his hands through his hair. "Why didn't you call an ambulance?"

She shook her head.

"Megan, why didn't you call someone?"

"I don't know."

"Because you've been drinking. Christ, I can smell it."

"I panicked," Megan said. "I was going to call an ambulance, but then Fiona showed up and I got scared and—"

"Who the hell is Fiona?"

"One of the neighbors," she said. "I didn't want her to know I was there when it happened. I didn't want anyone to blame me."

Tyler turned to face her, his eyes narrow.

"Blame you?"

She didn't say anything.

"Megan?" Tyler's voice was low. "Why would anyone blame you?"

"I don't know." She paused. "We were arguing, and there were these damn lawn gnomes. I threw one and—"

Her voice cracked, and she stopped.

"And what?"

"I didn't do anything." A wave of anger broke in the center of her chest and spread. "She was on the top of this ladder, and when I threw it, she ducked and—"

"Jesus, Megan."

"It wasn't my fault!" This time, her voice was loud. "She lost her balance and she fell. I never touched her."

She wanted to keep yelling, but Tyler was staring down at her, and she didn't recognize the look in his eyes.

Megan turned away. "I don't know what to do."

"We call the police, that's what we do."

"The police?"

"What do you think we're going to do? Ignore this and hope it goes away?"

"They'll blame me," she said. "It was an accident, but they'll blame me."

"A woman is dead, Megan. She's dead."

"I know she's dead!" Megan stopped and put a hand to her mouth, trying to calm down. But when she spoke again, her voice trembled. "I could go to prison."

The look in Tyler's eyes changed, and for a moment he just stood there. Then he moved toward the window and neither of them said anything.

"You're sure she's dead?" he asked.

"Jesus, Tyler."

"I mean it. Are you absolutely sure?"

"Yes, I'm sure," she said. "Go see for yourself if you don't believe me."

It wasn't a serious suggestion, but Megan could see that he was considering it. Eventually, he turned away from the window and nodded.

"Yeah, I'll go check."

"What? Wait—"

"If she's dead, we'll call the police and tell them I found her," he said. "They'll never have to know you were involved."

Megan felt a rush of joy and relief, but then she thought about Fiona and Mrs. Davidson, and the feeling faded fast.

"That won't work," she said. "They saw me."

"Who saw you?"

"Fiona and Edna next door," she said. "They saw me leaving her house. They know I was over there."

Tyler seemed to think about this. "Then if it comes up, you'll say you rang the bell and no one answered. You assumed she wasn't home and you left."

"But what if they—"

"They won't. Not if we do it this way."

"But—"

"If we call the police now and tell them what happened, they'll want to know why you waited so long." He shook his head. "No, this is our best choice."

"You want to lie to the police."

"No, but I also don't want to lose everything we have because you panicked." He paused. "I'll go over and ring the bell. Then I'll walk around to the garage and look inside."

"Are you sure?"

"You said it was an accident, right?"

"Yes, of course."

"She lost her balance and fell."

Megan nodded.

"Okay." He took a deep breath. "Then don't worry. It'll be fine."

Megan got up and followed him to the door. Before he walked out, she reached for his hand and pulled him toward her, wrapping her arms around him.

Tyler put one arm over her shoulder, but there was no strength in it, and he pulled away almost immediately.

"Stay here," he said. "I'll be right back."

Megan closed the door behind him, then went into the living room and stood at the front window. She watched him walk down the street and cross over. Then her stomach cramped, and she turned away.

She didn't want to see, so she went back to the couch and sat with her head in her hands.

And waited.

———

Megan didn't know how much time had passed, but she felt every second. After a while, she got up and looked out the window. Tyler was coming back, his head low as he made his way up the street.

She hurried to the front door, opening it right as he climbed the porch steps.

He didn't look at her when he came inside.

She started to say something, but then she noticed the look in his eyes and stopped. Tyler glanced at her and frowned.

Then he walked down the hall toward the kitchen.

Megan closed the door and followed.

She wanted to give him time, but the wait was eating at her.

She had to know what he'd seen.

Tyler grabbed a glass from the dish rack. He opened the cabinet above the refrigerator and took down a bottle of bourbon and poured. Then he set the bottle on the counter and drank, emptying the glass.

When he spoke, his voice sounded empty.

"I can't do this again, Megan. I just can't."

She frowned, stepped closer.

Tyler refilled the glass, took a sip.

"What are you talking about?" She reached out and touched his back, feeling him go tense. "Tyler?"

"I don't have it in me," he said. "I can't do it."

"Can't do what?"

He shook his head, didn't speak.

Megan hesitated, then whispered, "Did you see her?"

Tyler laughed under his breath, then turned to face her, his eyes sharp.

"Of course I saw her," he said. "She answered the goddamned door."

8

Megan didn't understand, and all she could do was stand there, staring up at him. Her throat was dry, and when she tried to speak, the words wouldn't come.

She told herself she hadn't heard him right.

The idea was enough for her to find her voice, but all she managed to say was "She what?"

Tyler looked at her, his eyes cold.

"She answered the door." His voice was calm. "What were you thinking? Why would you do this to me?"

Megan didn't know what to say. She kept waiting for all of it to make sense, but it didn't, and each second that passed only made it worse.

"What do you mean she answered the—"

"I mean she answered the goddamned door, Megan." Tyler's voice turned sharp. "How much clearer do I need to be?"

"That's not possible." She shook her head, looking up at him. "Tyler, I saw her die."

"You saw her die?" He lifted his glass and pointed in the direction of Rachel's house, splashing his drink on the floor, not noticing. "That's funny, because she's over there right now, and she's sure as hell not dead."

"I—" Her voice cracked. "I don't—"

"I don't understand you," he said. "I know you've had your problems with the woman, but this?"

"Tyler, I didn't—"

"This isn't normal, Megan. It's not healthy."

"I didn't make it up."

He opened his mouth to speak, but then something in his eyes changed, turned soft. He bit down on his lip and looked away, silent.

"You don't believe me," she said.

Tyler stared down at the glass in his hand, shook his head. "I can't go through this again. I can't. Are you this desperate for attention?"

A flash of anger burned through her, so strong she took a step back. "You think I made this up? For attention?"

"Then explain it to me," he said. "Because right now I don't know who you are."

"I'm not lying, Tyler." She tried to keep her voice down, but each word came out louder than the last. "I saw her fall. Her neck was broken."

"It's not broken now."

"I know what I saw!"

Tyler made a dismissive sound and lifted his drink. He drained it, then leaned against the counter. "Even now, this is some kind of game to you."

She stared at him, hard, then turned and walked out.

"Megan?"

He followed her down the hall. She could hear his footsteps behind her, but she didn't stop and she didn't slow down. When she got to the front door, she slipped on her red Chuck Taylors and walked outside.

"What are you doing?"

Megan ignored him. She went down the steps and across the yard and had just stepped into the street when she felt Tyler's hand on her arm, pulling her back.

Megan jerked away. "Don't touch me."

Tyler let go, and she kept walking.

He tried to step around her, but she ducked past him, moving down the street toward Rachel's house.

"Megan, wait." Tyler ran in front of her, cutting her off.

She stopped walking and stared up at him. "I know what I saw, and I'm not making it up. I'm not crazy."

"You can't go over there," he said. "You can't drag the neighbors into your personal shit."

Megan made a low growling sound and pushed past him.

Tyler reached out, grabbing her arm again. This time, she screamed at him. "Goddamn it, let go of me!"

Her voice echoed through the neighborhood, surprising

her. All at once the situation came into focus, and she glanced around at the houses lining the street. She didn't see anyone, but she couldn't shake the feeling that they were being observed.

Tyler must've felt it too, because when he spoke, his voice was even and soft. "Megan, please. Come back inside."

Megan's entire body was shaking, and she couldn't make it stop. "I know what I saw, Tyler."

"Please." He spoke through clenched teeth. "Not out here. Not right now."

The air suddenly turned cold, and she looked around at the oddly silent audience of houses.

Tyler held out his hand. "Come home, please."

This time, she took his hand.

―――――

Tyler closed the front door and locked the bolt.

"I'd ask if you'd like a drink, but I'm guessing you've had enough."

It sounded like a joke, but Megan knew him well enough to know that it wasn't. Either way, she was beyond caring.

"How about a cup of coffee?" he asked.

She shook her head, kicked off her shoes, and started for the stairs.

"Where are you going?"

"Upstairs," she said. "I'm going to take a hot bath and go to bed."

"We need to talk about this." He followed her to the foot of the stairs. "I'm worried about you."

Megan stopped halfway up and looked down at him. He had one hand on the banister, one foot on the first step.

"What else do you want me to say?" she asked. "I know what I saw. I'm not making it up."

"Okay, I believe you."

She shook her head. "No, you don't, and that's the problem."

"I believe you believe it."

Megan laughed, but there was no humor in it. "What the hell does that even mean?"

"It means you saw something. Maybe you thought—"

She held up a hand. "Just stop."

Tyler exhaled, slowly. "Megs, Rachel Addison is alive, and she's inside her house right now. So whatever you think you saw, it obviously wasn't what you thought."

Megan stood there, staring at him, but there was nothing else to say. Every part of her was exhausted, and all she wanted to do was sleep.

She turned and continued up the stairs. "I'm going to bed."

"This isn't something we can ignore," Tyler said. "We're going to have to talk about it."

"Not tonight."

She went into the bathroom and locked the door. Then she turned on the water in the tub and closed the drain. She slipped her shirt over her head and leaned against the sink, staring at her reflection in the mirror.

It was her face, but it wasn't her.

Megan tried to replay everything that'd happened. She wanted to believe she was wrong, that she'd made a mistake, that Rachel really was still alive.

But everything inside of her knew better.

She stayed at the mirror until the steam clouded the glass. Then she took a pack of matches from the medicine cabinet and lit one of the candles on the counter before getting undressed and stepping into the tub.

The water was hot, and it burned her skin, but as she closed her eyes and slid under the surface, she barely felt a thing.

PART II

9

*I*n the dream, Megan is standing in her old apartment in Chicago. She's alone, and the room is filled with a deep red light. All her furniture is missing, and there are no curtains on the windows. The jeweled city lights are gone, turning the glass into depthless black mirrors.

She stares at her reflection.

Then her focus shifts, and Megan sees the ghost of a child standing behind her, a girl, motionless, like a doll. Her dark hair is long, and she's wearing a thin white nightgown that falls to just below her bruised knees.

Her face is lost in shadows.

Megan spins around, fast, but the girl is gone.

The front door is standing open, and the pale fluorescent light from the hallway buzzes, calling for her.

She steps through, but she doesn't see the girl.

The hallway is long and lined with dozens of numberless wooden doors. The carpet is a heavy sea green and dotted with candy-yellow snakes that seem to shimmer and move under the watery light.

Behind her, Megan hears a door slam shut. She turns and follows the sound to a metal door, pushes through, and steps out onto the rooftop.

The girl is there, standing along the far edge. Her back is turned, and her dark hair moves slowly from side to side, drifting like seaweed in the cool night air. She has one arm outstretched, pointing toward the darkened Chicago skyline.

Megan feels a twist of panic deep inside, and she moves closer. She tries to tell the girl to step away from the edge, that it's not safe, but she has no voice.

The girl doesn't move.

As Megan gets closer, she can hear the wind sighing through the maze of empty streets below, while above them, the sky spins in an endless tapestry of starlight.

She looks down at the girl and follows the line of her arm toward the black skyline and the Sears Tower rising in the distance, a shadow among shadows.

At first, there's nothing.

Then she sees it: a single pulsing blue light, faint and far-away, the color of arctic ice. It pans over the city like the call of a lighthouse, growing brighter and stronger with each turn.

It's impossible to look away.

Megan watches as the light crawls across the abandoned city, reaching down into its concrete canyons, and covering rows upon rows of dark, haunted windows.

The closer it comes, the calmer she feels.

Next to her, the girl is still and quiet, her arm outstretched toward the growing blue light. Megan wants to reach out to her and tell her that everything is okay, that it's all as it should be, but she can't move.

She can't turn away.

When the light reaches the river, the blue reflects off the wa-

ter in a shatter of silver that tears through the city like an explosion of glass. The light grows, rising and folding over them in a wave, scattering the world into the wind, and then up into the silent, swirling sky.

And then there is nothing.

———

When Megan opened her eyes, the bedroom was bright. The curtains were partly open, and the warm morning sun shone across the foot of the bed in a thin golden line. The dream was still fresh in her mind, and she tried to hold on to it, but eventually the images faded, slipping into daylight.

She sat up and looked over at Tyler's side of the bed.

The sheets were untouched.

Megan let her head fall back on the pillow, and she closed her eyes. Her mouth was dry, and she could taste the wine from the night before in her throat. The smell of her own breath made her stomach turn.

She needed to move.

When she felt ready, she swung her legs out from under the covers and sat on the edge of the bed, cradling her head in her hands as the room tilted around her.

Eventually, she got up and made her way to the bathroom. She turned on the faucet and let the water run cold. Then she cupped her hands, took a long drink, and scrubbed her face, trying to clear the fog from her head.

Slowly, everything came back to her.

When she turned off the water, her hands were shaking. She squeezed them into fists until they stopped. Then she went back into the bedroom and got dressed.

She could hear the rumble of the lawn mower starting up outside, and she crossed to the window and looked out. Tyler was pushing the mower from one side of the lawn to the other. He had on a thin white T-shirt that clung to his skin and seemed to glow in the sunlight.

Megan watched him for a few minutes, thinking about everything that'd happened the night before, going over it again and again in her mind. Then she turned away from the window and walked downstairs to the kitchen.

Tyler always made coffee on the weekends, but this time the pot was empty, so she made it herself. While she waited for it to brew, she thought about what she was going to say to him when he came inside.

Last night had been the first time he hadn't come to bed after a fight, and while she didn't want to read anything into it, it was hard not to.

She knew what he wanted.

He wanted her to apologize and say she'd made it all up, and part of her thought that would be easier, but she couldn't do it. She knew what'd happened in that garage, and she wasn't going to pretend she didn't.

Megan tried to think of how she could convince him she was telling the truth, but it was pointless. Whatever Tyler had seen at Rachel's house, it wasn't what she'd seen, and there was nothing either of them could say that would make a difference. If she wanted him to believe her, she needed proof.

———

By the time the coffee finished brewing, Tyler was done mowing the lawn and Megan still didn't know what she was going to say to him. She took her yellow coffee cup from the dish drainer and filled it. Then, as she walked out to the living room, she noticed a brochure sitting on the counter.

Megan picked it up and sipped her coffee.

The photo on the front showed a young couple standing together on an ocean pier under a peaceful blue sky. They were staring up at each other with wide, smiling eyes.

The words printed under the photo read:

Hansen Institute Family Counseling

Megan set her coffee cup on the counter and bit down hard on the insides of her cheeks. She counted a few deep breaths, then carried the brochure down the hall and out the front door into the light.

Tyler was in the yard, kneeling over the mower. He had it on its side, and he was scraping thick clumps of grass from around the blade with a short-handled knife.

"Hey."

Tyler glanced at her over his shoulder. Then he turned back to the mower and said, "How'd you sleep?"

For an instant, all the hurt and disappointment disappeared. The memory of the blue dream flashed through her mind, but it was gone as quickly as it'd come.

"It was lonely," she said. "I missed you."

"I thought it would be better if I slept on the couch in the office."

She waited for him to say more, or to at least look at her, but he didn't. Megan stared down at the brochure in her hand and let the silence between them grow until she couldn't take it anymore.

"I assume you left this for me?"

Tyler stopped cleaning and glanced back.

She held it up for him to see. "Subtle, by the way."

He sighed and dropped the knife. When he stood, he took a rag from his pocket and stared off toward the ridge in the distance, wiping his hands clean. "I think I'm finally starting to see how unhappy you are here."

The comment surprised her, and Megan thought about her response before she spoke. "I miss Chicago, that's all."

"There's obviously more to it than that."

"If you think how I feel about this place has anything to do with what I saw last night, you're wrong."

"What you think you saw."

Megan took a breath and reminded herself to stay calm. Then she said, "You really don't believe me, do you?"

"How can I?" He motioned toward the street. "I saw her myself."

"You saw her? You talked to her?"

"We didn't have a conversation, but I rang the bell and she opened the door enough to look out and see me."

"What did you say to her?"

"Nothing. It was late and I felt like an idiot. I apologized for bothering her, and I came home."

Megan looked over at Rachel's house. The curtains were all closed, and it occurred to her that this was the first morning she could remember that Rachel wasn't outside in her garden. She thought about mentioning this to Tyler, but decided not to.

It would've only made things worse.

"We should talk about counseling."

"There's nothing to talk about."

"I think there is." He pointed to the brochure in her hand. "It helped after your mom died, and it could help now. I'll even go along if you think—"

"This is completely different."

Tyler hesitated. "All I'm saying is we should see what they have to offer. It won't hurt."

"No."

"Megs, I really think—"

"I'm not going, so drop it."

Tyler frowned, then he knelt down and picked up the knife. "I'm going down to the plaza when I'm done here. If you need anything, let me know."

"I'll go with you," Megan said. "I want to see if—"

"I think I'd rather go alone."

"Are you—" Her throat closed on the words. She swallowed, tried again. "Are you serious?"

"I need some time."

Megan stood there for a moment, not knowing what to say. Then she turned and went back inside. As she closed the door, she felt something break in the center of her chest, and she had a sudden, overwhelming desire to run outside and wrap her arms around Tyler's neck and tell him she was sorry, and that she'd talk to a counselor if they could just stop fighting.

Whatever he wanted.

Then she remembered the sound of Rachel's neck snapping as she fell, and the way her eyes dimmed to gray when she stopped breathing. And no matter how hard she tried, she couldn't make the memory go away.

When Tyler came in, Megan was on the couch in the living room. She heard him slide his keys from the bowl by the door, but he didn't walk out.

She could feel him watching her.

"Megan," he said. "Don't go over there."

She didn't look at him.

"Promise me you'll leave her alone?"

Megan's jaw ached, and she realized she was grinding her teeth. She didn't want to promise anything. She had to know what he'd seen, and that meant going over and seeing Rachel for herself.

"Megan, please. Promise me."

She looked up at him, her face set and cold.

"Fine," she said. "I won't go over there."

"Thank you."

Tyler hesitated, as if wanting to say more, but instead he walked out. A minute later, she heard his car door slam and the engine start up before fading away down the street.

Megan leaned back, feeling the world go black.

10

I'm not crazy.

She repeated the words to herself, over and over, as she paced through the house. The brochure Tyler had left for her was on the coffee table, but she couldn't bring herself to look at it. After her mother died, it'd been good to talk to someone, to come to terms with the loss, but this wasn't the same. Counseling wasn't going to help her this time, and she knew there was nothing written in that brochure that would change her mind.

I'm not crazy.

Tyler had been gone for hours, and the more time that passed, the more she wondered if he was coming back at all, or if she'd finally pushed him away for good.

It was strange, but part of her actually understood.

The last several months had been tough on them both. Part of it was Tyler's new position at the Institute, and part of it was the loneliness and isolation she felt living in Willow Ridge; but there was something else there, too, something just under the surface that Megan couldn't quite see.

They'd lost something when they left Chicago, and they both sensed it, but neither of them could explain it.

One day it'd been there, and then it just wasn't.

And in its place, a hollow spot.

Tyler thought it was a breakdown, that emotions left over from her mother's death were resurfacing, and that she was being stubborn by refusing to talk to someone. But he was wrong. She wasn't having a breakdown, not this time, and she wasn't going to give in.

Walking back to the living room, she glanced at the grand-father clock. It was later than she'd thought, and once again the idea that Tyler might not be coming home sunk into her chest like a blade, cold and deep.

The pain was real, making it hard to breathe.

Eventually the feeling passed, replaced by guilt and tears. Megan grabbed the brochure and skimmed through the promises inside. Then she dropped it back on the coffee table, wiped her cheeks with her fingertips, and stared out the front window at the blue sky, and the yellow sun, and the bright green world.

I'm not crazy.

Until she saw for herself that Rachel was alive, she wasn't about to admit that she'd made a mistake, or that what she saw never actually happened. She wasn't going to lie on a couch and talk to a complete stranger about it, and there was no way she'd say she made it up as some desperate cry for attention.

That only left one option.

She had to break her promise to Tyler.

———

Megan stepped out onto the porch, forcing herself to not look at Rachel's house. Instead, she focused on the curved grain of the wood on the steps, and on the scatter of cut grass along the sidewalk as she passed by. She lost herself in the smell of the lilacs, and she let the steady hum of the bees fill her, blocking out the rest of the world.

But eventually, she had to look.

From a distance, the house was quiet. The curtains, normally open to the sun, were closed, and the only movement she saw was the gentle, windblown sway of the roses, and the silver shimmer of the leaves in the trees.

A red pickup truck turned the corner at the end of the street, heading toward her. As it passed, the driver, who Megan didn't recognize, lifted two fingers off the steering wheel in a lazy hello.

Megan pretended not to notice.

When she got to the corner, she looked up at the Institute at the top of the ridge. The sun reflected bright off the long rows of black glass, blinding her. She turned away and thought about Tyler and wondered if she was doing the right thing.

What exactly am I doing?

She realized she didn't have a plan.

Was she just going to walk up to the front door and ring the bell? If so, what was she going to say if Rachel actually answered? What would Rachel say to her?

And what would happen if Rachel didn't answer?

What if she went around the house and found Rachel lying where she'd left her in the garage, her neck still twisted, her skin now bloated and blue?

"Stop it."

The sound of her own voice brought her back, and she pressed her fingers against the side of her head and took a long, slow breath. She reminded herself that no matter what happened, it was going to be okay. Whatever she found, it wouldn't matter.

All she needed were answers.

Megan stepped off the curb and crossed over to the sidewalk on the other side of the street. She followed the long straight line of concrete toward the horizon and saw several sprinklers turning over lawns in the distance, each one creating the illusion of rainbows in the sunlight.

She stopped outside of Rachel's house and stared up at the front door. Somewhere, far off, she heard a dog bark, then another.

Her legs wouldn't move.

All she had to do was walk up the path and ring the bell,

and everything would be resolved one way or another.

But she couldn't do it.

Instead, she looked down and kept walking, past Rachel's house, toward the garage. Her chest ached, and she cursed herself under her breath for being such a coward.

When she reached the edge of the driveway, Megan stopped. She knew that if she wanted to make things better with Tyler, she had to know what he'd seen.

She had to see it for herself.

Slowly, she started back toward the walkway leading up to the front door. She'd only taken a couple steps when she heard something move along the side of the garage.

Megan listened.

At first, there was nothing.

Then she heard it again.

The sound was quiet, but it was there, a slow rustling, a scraping followed by a dull tap.

A rabbit?

She told herself to walk around the garage and see what was on the other side, but it seemed like an eternity before her legs responded and started moving.

She stayed focused on the shadowed path running between the garage and the tall row of hedges, and each step she took revealed a little more. She saw the familiar pale white light shining out from the side door, and heard the scraping sound again, the tapping.

She held her breath, her lungs burning as she pushed herself forward, straining to see.

A flash of gold. . . A dress . . . A shadow . . .

"Hey there."

Megan spun around, her voice coming out in a short scream. She felt the ground shift under her, and then a hand on her arm, steadying her.

"Oh God, I'm so sorry."

Fiona was standing in front of her. The look on her face was a perfect mix of pity and laughter.

Megan's heart was in her throat, and the world was spinning. She couldn't catch her breath.

"I was calling you from across the street," Fiona said, trying not to smile. "Didn't you hear me?"

"What?"

Megan pulled her arm away and looked back toward the side of the garage. The light was out, and the door was closed. Whatever she'd seen, it was gone.

"Are you okay?"

Megan didn't answer.

Her mind was racing, trying to piece together what she'd seen, what she thought she'd seen. Her hands were numb, cramped into fists, but she didn't feel the pain until Fiona stepped in and took them in hers.

"Hey, what's wrong?" she asked. "What's going on?"

"Nothing," Megan said. "I just—"

She looked past Fiona toward the front of Rachel's house. For an instant, she thought she saw one of the curtains move, but she couldn't be sure.

"You're shaking," Fiona said. "Look at your hands."

Megan glanced down and turned them over, stretching her fingers out. There were tiny half-moons dug into her palms. A few of them were bleeding.

"Come on," Fiona said. "I'll walk you home."

"No!" Megan's voice came out loud, surprising them both. "I can't go back there. I can't."

Fiona stared at her, the humor in her eyes long gone. "In that case," she said, "you'll come home with me."

Megan wanted to tell her no, that she'd be fine, and that she didn't need her help. But when she started to speak, she began to cry.

Fiona stepped in and wrapped her arms around her.

Megan didn't want to cry, but the tears wouldn't stop. Eventually, Fiona put an arm over her shoulder and led her away.

Megan apologized, told her that she was embarrassed.

Fiona smiled.

"Don't worry," she said, pulling her in tighter. "This is all perfectly normal."

11

I 've got green or Earl Grey."
Fiona leaned out of the kitchen and held up two boxes, one yellow and one a pale green.

"Green is fine," Megan said. "Thank you."

Fiona disappeared back into the kitchen, and Megan heard the familiar sounds of cabinets and drawers, cups and spoons, water running and tea bags pulled from wrappers. She waited for the questions, like why was she standing outside Rachel's house and whether she was okay.

But Fiona didn't ask anything.

Instead, she hummed a soft song that Megan couldn't quite place, and she didn't say a word.

For that, Megan was grateful.

"I picked up a new kettle at the plaza the other day," Fiona said. "I haven't had a chance to use it yet, so I'm glad you're here. You can be my lab rat."

"I don't mind."

Megan got up and wandered around the living room, looking at the furniture and the art and the flow of the room. Fiona's house was the mirror image of hers, and it was a little unsettling at first. Having the kitchen on the right, and the stairs on the left felt unnatural. But the biggest difference, and the one that stood out to her the most, was the view from the front window.

Fiona's window faced south, overlooking the street and the grove of willow trees running along the base of the ridge. There were a few houses in the way, but if she stood in the right place, she could block them out and have an unbroken view of the dense, swaying forest.

In the kitchen, the kettle whistled and Fiona said, "Looks like it works. Experiment, successful."

Megan knew she should say something to be polite, but she was lost in the view and it was hard to break away.

"Your view is incredible."

"It's about the only thing in this place I wouldn't change." Fiona's voice got louder as she came into the room. "If you stand in the corner, you don't have to look at any of the houses across—" She saw Megan and stopped. "Never mind. Looks like you figured it out."

Fiona was carrying a wooden tray holding two teacups, a sugar bowl, and a teapot—all of it blue-and-white china. She set the tray on the coffee table, then crossed the room and stood next to Megan.

"When I first moved here, I put a chair right in this spot, and I'd sit for hours and stare out at those trees." Fiona exhaled, slowly. "There's something so calming about weeping willows, don't you think?"

"They're beautiful."

"Did you know they used to grow wild around here?"

"No, I didn't."

"The Institute had them removed to clear the land for these houses." She frowned. "At least they spared a few."

Megan turned to face her. "I want to thank you for—"

Fiona raised one hand, stopping her. "Let's not do that. Everyone has a hard time adjusting to this place at first. You have no reason to apologize."

"I guess I should feel better knowing I'm not the only one."

"Not by a long shot."

"Still, I bet not many have breakdowns in the middle of the street."

Fiona laughed, but not at her. "You might be surprised."

Eventually, they turned away from the window and sat on the couch. Fiona poured the tea, and after a few awkward moments, they began to talk.

Not once did Fiona ask why she was upset, or what she was doing outside Rachel's house. She didn't mention Tyler, or the long hours he spent away from home, and Megan didn't say a word about what'd happened in Rachel's garage.

Instead, they talked about art, their favorite books, and about how bright the stars shone out there in the lowlands, so far removed from the rest of the world.

Mostly, they talked about finding peace in change.

At some point, Megan glanced out the window and saw the sun had gone down, and that several hours had drifted away.

"I didn't realize it was so late."

Fiona turned to the window. "Funny how the days slip by, isn't it?"

Megan offered to help clean up, but Fiona refused.

"This was nice," Megan said. "Thank you."

"Anytime."

Fiona walked Megan to the door and stood with her on the porch, holding out her arms. They hugged, and for the first time in a long time, Megan didn't feel alone.

Before she started down the steps toward the yard, she turned back.

"Just so you know, the reason I was upset this afternoon wasn't because of Tyler." She hesitated. "At least not entirely."

Fiona leaned against the doorframe and slipped her hands into the front pockets of her jeans. "I'm glad to hear that."

"We're not seeing eye to eye on a few things right now, but that's not the entire reason I was upset," she said. "I don't want how you found me this afternoon to color your opinion of him."

"It won't."

"It's just, you didn't ask about it, so I thought . . ."

"It's not my place to ask, but I'm happy you told me." Fiona leaned forward and looked around at the other houses. "This place isn't easy, Megan, but it helps when you have someone who cares, and you do."

"Even if he's not always around?"

Fiona smiled. "Even then."

———

Walking home along the sidewalk, Megan watched the fireflies drifting gently over the neighborhood lawns and thought about Tyler. Fiona was right. As bad as things were, it helped to have someone around who cared.

She hoped he'd be home when she got there.

All she wanted was a chance to talk to him, to tell him that they could work through this together. If that meant counseling, then maybe she would bend a little.

She wasn't going to change her story about what happened to Rachel, but she wasn't going to let it destroy her marriage, either.

As Megan turned the corner onto her street, she held her breath. When she saw her house, the windows lit and Tyler's car parked in the driveway, it took everything she had not to run the rest of the way.

Inside, the house smelled sweet.

There was a soft breeze blowing through from the open windows, and a vase of white tulips on the dining room table. Tyler was outside on the back porch, sitting alone on one of the patio chairs with a drink in his hand.

Megan slid the screen door open and stepped out.

He glanced back, set his glass down, and stood up.

For a moment, neither of them spoke.

"You're here," Megan said. "I wasn't sure you would be."

"Why would you think that?"

The question carried weight, and she didn't answer. Instead, she motioned back toward the house and said, "Are the flowers for me?"

"A peace offering."

She smiled, didn't speak.

"I didn't handle things last night as well as I could have," he said. "And I'm sorry."

"You don't have to say that."

"I still don't understand," he said. "But the way I went about it, and some of the things I said—"

"We don't have to talk about last night."

Tyler nodded. "I could've handled it better."

Megan stepped closer and angled up to kiss him. For one brief moment, when their lips touched, all the bad thoughts slipped away. She felt like herself again, and for the first time all day, Rachel Addison didn't exist.

———

For the next couple days, things were quiet. Tyler went to work, and Fiona talked Megan into joining her on her daily walks through the neighborhood.

It didn't take much for Megan to agree.

Out of all the people she'd met since moving to Willow Ridge, Fiona was the only one who seemed real to her, and Megan always felt better when she was around.

She still kept an eye on Rachel's house, but she didn't mention her, or what'd happened that night, to anyone. One morning Tyler had found her staring out the window at Rachel's house, but to his credit, he didn't say a word.

In a way, they were both still shocked by what'd happened. It'd been their biggest fight since leaving Chicago, and it'd left them both feeling raw.

Neither of them wanted to make waves.

So they moved on, slipping back into old patterns and routines, leaving all the ugly thoughts behind.

At first it seemed to work, and they were happy.

But then, three days after Megan watched her die, Rachel Addison opened her front door and stepped outside.

12

Megan was driving home from the plaza when she saw her, moving slowly across her yard toward her rosebushes.

At first, she hardly recognized her.

Rachel was wearing the same gold sundress from the night in the garage, but one of the shoulder straps had been torn free, and there was a dark, greasy stain along the back. Her hair fell around her shoulders, tangled and caked with dirt.

Megan hit the brakes, hard, and the car skidded to a stop in the middle of the street. She was aware of the low death rattle coming from the Corsica's engine, and the rapid pass of her breath in her throat, but she barely noticed either.

All she could do was stare.

Rachel was carrying her pink-handled pruning shears in one hand and the white plastic bucket in the other, and when she got to the rosebushes, she stopped and dropped the bucket on the grass. It hit the ground at an angle and tipped onto its side, but Rachel didn't seem to notice.

Megan watched as she knelt in front of the rosebush, reached in bare-handed, and randomly cut away one of the branches, roses and all. Then she dropped the severed branch on the ground next to the overturned bucket and reached for another.

She cut them out, one at a time.

After a while, Megan's hands started to ache, and she realized she was squeezing the steering wheel. She pried her fingers loose and shook her hands out, rubbing one with the other.

Behind her, someone honked.

Megan glanced up in the rearview and waved them by.

The driver shook his head and sped around her. She felt him staring at her as he passed, but she didn't care.

She didn't even look at him.

Her focus was on Rachel, kneeling in her garden, and slowly cutting a hole through the center of her rosebush.

After the second car passed, Megan realized she was drawing attention, so she drove to her house and parked in the garage. But instead of going inside, she walked down and watched Rachel from the end of her driveway.

Then the phone rang.

Megan considered letting it go, but then she thought it might be Tyler, so she ran inside and picked it up.

It was Fiona.

"Bad news," she said. "Looks like I'm not going to be able to go on our walk in the morning."

Megan carried the phone into the living room and looked out the front window at Rachel. "What happened?"

"I have to go in early tomorrow," she said. "One of the units in my section is on the fritz, and I have to arrange to get it taken off the grid."

"I thought you were an administrator?"

"I am, and that makes me a supervisor. I'm responsible for all the test units in my section." She paused. "It's a wide umbrella. Not all that interesting."

Megan knew from hearing Tyler talk about his job that she was probably right, but she didn't say that to her.

"Too bad you can't go," Megan said. "I was looking forward to it."

"Go by yourself."

"It's not the same."

"Fresh air is good for the mind," Fiona said. "Don't let me keep you."

"I'll think about it."

Outside, Rachel stood up and grabbed the overturned bucket, ignoring the large pile of cut branches lying on the grass. She carried the empty bucket back to the garage and disappeared from view behind the hedges.

"Listen," Megan said. "Can we talk later? I just got back from the store, and I—"

"Of course." Fiona cut her off. "I only wanted to tell you

the bad news about tomorrow. Sorry again for skipping out on you like this."

After they hung up, Megan stayed at the window and waited for Rachel to return. When she didn't, Megan carried the phone into the kitchen and set it in the cradle. Then she went outside and walked down the street, heading for Rachel's house.

Megan didn't think about what she was doing, only that she had to have a closer look. She had to see Rachel up close, had to talk to her, had to hear her voice. Because even though she'd seen her outside with her own eyes, part of her still didn't believe she was real.

When she got to Rachel's house, she went around the side of the garage and looked down the path. Rachel wasn't there, and the side door was closed.

Megan cut across the yard to the porch and climbed the steps to the front door and rang the bell.

She heard the familiar two-toned chime from deep inside the house and felt her first real tinge of fear. She did her best to push it down and bury it.

No one answered the door.

Megan rang again, and this time she stepped closer and listened for movement inside.

Nothing.

Megan stood on the porch, waiting. She stared down at the two ceramic turtles beside the door and tried to figure out what to do next.

She could hear Tyler's voice in her head telling her to go home, to leave Rachel alone, but it was too late for that. She knew if she went home, she'd never have the courage to come back, and that wasn't an option.

She had to know.

Megan stepped off the porch and crossed the yard to the side of the house and stopped next to the pile of newly cut branches lying on the grass next to the rosebush. She bent forward and examined the hole in the center of the bush, and once again she heard Tyler's voice, whispering to her, telling her that it was none of her business.

This time, she almost listened.

Instead, she turned away from the rosebushes and walked around to the side of the house and tried to look in through the dining room window. There was a break in the curtains, but it was too high up for her to see, so she looked around the empty yard for something to stand on.

Then she remembered.

Megan ran back to the porch and picked up one of the ceramic turtles. It was heavier than she'd expected, and the muscles in her arms burned as she carried it to the side of the house and set it under the window.

Once it was in place, she stepped up and looked through the break in the curtains, into the dining room.

At first, she didn't understand what she was seeing.

The large oak table had been pushed sideways against the wall, and all the chairs had been overturned. There was broken china scattered across the floor, and one corner of the Persian rug looked black and charred.

On the other side of the room, she could see the bar-top counter that separated the dining room from the kitchen. The surface was covered with dirt, and behind it, the refrigerator was open, its contents spilling out, rotting on the floor.

"What in the hell?"

Megan pressed her face against the glass, cupping her hands around her eyes to block the glare from the sun. It helped, and she stood there for a long time, trying to make sense of the scene.

But she couldn't.

She was still focused on the room when she felt something soft, like a cold breath, brush against the back of her neck.

She spun around, fast.

Rachel was standing behind her, hand outstretched, fingers reaching toward her.

Megan jerked away. Her foot slipped off the back of the turtle, and she fell, landing hard in the grass. An electric jolt shivered along her arm, from her elbow to her shoulder. There was no pain, but when she tried to push herself up, her arm folded under her.

Megan rolled onto her back and pushed away with her legs until she could get her feet under her and stand up.

Rachel watched, silent.

"I rang the bell," Megan said, backing away. "No one answered, so I came around here. I didn't mean to—"

Rachel stepped closer.

There was a deep black bruise on her cheek, and the white of her right eye was solid red. Megan could see angry scratches and cuts on her hands and up her arms, and there were several bald patches on her scalp, as if entire chunks of hair had been ripped away.

Megan tried to tell her again that she was sorry, but before she could get the words out, the smell hit hard.

Ripe and rotting.

It rolled off Rachel in waves, and Megan took another step back, trying to breathe, her eyes watering.

Rachel moved with her, matching each step.

Megan wanted to run, but her legs wouldn't go. When she opened her mouth, the words stuck in her throat, and all she could do was stare.

Finally, she found her voice.

"What happened to you?"

Rachel paused midstep.

Megan watched as the edges of her lips split apart, curling both up and down at the same time, showing a row of perfectly white teeth.

It took a minute before she understood.

She's smiling at me.

Again, the urge to run tore through her.

Megan turned and moved, fast, across the yard and back toward the sidewalk and into the street. Once she was on her side of the road, she glanced over her shoulder.

Rachel was following her.

Moving slowly, smiling.

Megan ran the rest of the way to her house, her breath coming out in small cries. When she reached her front door, she looked over her shoulder and saw Rachel cutting across the street, her eyes focused on her.

Megan hurried inside and shut the door. She pressed against it and stared out through the peephole, her breath quick, her heart beating hard in her chest.

It seemed like forever before Rachel came into view.

She moved slowly, stopping at the end of the walkway and looking up at the house, her gold sundress fluttering gently in the wind, the smile wide on her face.

Megan leaned back against the door. Her heart was pounding so hard that her ribs ached, and she couldn't catch her breath. For a moment, the floor seemed to fall away underneath her, and she bent forward, hands on her knees, trying to calm down. *Deep, easy breaths.*

Eventually, she felt her mind begin to settle, and her pulse start to slow. When she was steady enough, she stood up and looked out the peephole.

Rachel was standing at the foot of the steps.

Megan jumped away, her hands pressed against her lips, holding back a scream.

The room was silent.

Then she heard footsteps outside the door, moving slowly up onto the porch.

Megan wanted to run.

A voice in her head screamed at her, telling her to get out of the house, to go through the kitchen and out the back, and to keep running until she was far, far away.

But her legs wouldn't move, and all she could do was stand there and stare at the closed door.

Several seconds went by before she noticed the door was unlocked.

Megan made a sharp sound and lurched forward. She fumbled for the lock, turned it, and heard the bolt click into place. Then she stepped back, her legs trembling under her, and listened for movement.

There was nothing.

Slowly, Megan inched closer, forcing herself to breathe. When she reached the door, she leaned in and looked out through the peephole.

Rachel was looking in from the other side.

Megan bit the insides of her cheeks, hard, and this time when the voice in her head screamed at her, telling her to get out of the house, she listened.

She was about to run when something changed.

Rachel's body seemed to stiffen, and she turned away from the door. She paused for a moment, then walked down the porch steps and along the path toward the street. When she reached the sidewalk, she turned right and headed home.

She never looked back.

Once Rachel was gone, Megan felt the strength in her legs drain away, and she slid down to the floor. There were tears running along her cheeks, and she wiped them away before pulling her legs up to her chest and wrapping her arms around her knees, squeezing them tight.

It was a long time before the shaking stopped.

13

M egan took her suitcase from the top shelf of the closet and opened it on the bed. She went to the dresser and started pulling clothes from the drawers. She only needed enough for a few days. Anything else she could pick up on the road, or back in Chicago.

All that mattered was getting away.

Once she finished packing, Megan carried the suitcase downstairs and set it by the front door. Then she went into the kitchen and took a pen and notepad from the drawer and sat at the dining room table.

At the top of the page, she wrote:

Tyler,

And stopped.

She'd thought writing the note would be easy, but as she stared down at the blank page, she realized that she had no idea what to say. There was so much to tell him, and she knew she couldn't put it all down in a letter.

She decided to keep it simple.

Under his name, she wrote:

I think we both knew this was coming for a while now, and I hope you're not too surprised that I've decided to leave. All I can say is that I'm sorry.

You should know that my decision has nothing to do with you, and everything to do with this new life and my place in it. It's become obvious to me over the past few months that I'm not the type of person who can live here, and for that I'm truly sorry.

So I'm going home.

I believe it's the best thing for me, and for both of us.

I'll call you once I get to the city and let you know where I'll be staying. I'm going to try and find a place in our old neighborhood. It won't be the same without you, but it's all I know. I hope you decide to join me.

I'll be waiting.

I love you.

Megan read the note over twice before signing it. Then she tore the page out, folded it in half, and set it on the kitchen counter.

She paused.

Seeing the note sitting there touched something inside of her, and she allowed herself a minute to take a step back and think about Tyler and how her leaving was going to affect him. She didn't know if she was making the right choice, or if she could really drive away and leave him behind without seeing him one more time.

Megan picked up the note and read it over again.

No, it wasn't enough.

Tyler deserved better, but she didn't know how she could make him understand. The last time they'd talked about Rachel, it'd almost broken them. If she brought her up again, told him what'd happened, all he'd hear was that Rachel caught her looking in her window and chased her off.

Nothing else she had to say would matter.

And then the fighting would start again, spiraling away from them both, neither willing to bend, and this time she wasn't sure they'd survive.

Still, he deserved more than a note.

It occurred to her that maybe this time he'd understand. He knew how unhappy she was living in Willow Ridge, and she thought if she was honest and told him she couldn't stay, maybe he'd accept it. She knew he wouldn't be happy, but at least she wouldn't be sneaking away while he was at work.

It was a small chance, but still a chance.

Megan glanced down at the note in her hand, hesitated, and then crumpled it into a ball and tossed it into the trash under the sink. She put the pen and notebook back in the drawer, then walked down the hall to the front door.

She took her suitcase and started up the stairs to the bedroom to unpack. She'd only taken a few steps when the image of Rachel following her home flashed in her mind.

Megan went back down.

She set the suitcase by the front door and pulled out two days' worth of clothes. Then she took a day bag from the closet, stuffed the clothes inside, and carried it out to the garage.

She opened the Corsica's trunk and set the bag inside.

It wasn't much, but knowing it was there in case she needed to leave in a hurry made her feel better.

———

That night, Tyler came home late.

Megan was in bed, but every time she closed her eyes, all she saw was Rachel's bruised face, making it impossible to sleep.

Tyler moved softly through the room, and for a while she let him. Eventually, she said, "It's okay. I'm awake."

"Sorry," he said. "I was trying to be quiet."

"It wasn't you."

"Is everything okay?"

She told him it was, then said, "I can't sleep."

Tyler sat next to her on the bed, and she felt the mattress give under his weight. He put a hand on her hip.

"Want to talk?"

She knew this was her chance, and every part of her wanted to tell him what'd happened, how she'd almost left, but when she tried, the words wouldn't come.

"Megs, what's wrong?"

"Nothing," she said. "Just tired."

Tyler leaned in and kissed her head. Then he got up and finished getting ready for bed. When he slid in next to her and put his arm around her shoulder, Megan pushed back against him and felt his body envelop hers.

It almost made her happy she'd decided to stay.

"You're shaking," Tyler said. "Are you cold?"

Megan wiped the tears from her cheeks. "No, I'm not cold."

For a while, they were both quiet.

Then Tyler said, "You think I can't tell when you're upset, but I can."

The comment surprised her, but she did her best not to show it. Instead, she whispered, "I know."

"You can talk to me," he said. "About anything."

Megan thought about this, wondering if it was true. She didn't believe it was, but she knew he did, and maybe that was good enough.

"What if I wanted to talk about going back home?"

"To Chicago?"

She nodded, silent.

"Then I'd tell you I have good news," he said. "I put in the request for time off today, and as soon as it clears, we're all set. We'll take a few days and—"

"Not a trip." She rolled over and faced him. "What if I wanted to go back home for good?"

It was too dark to see his face, but Megan felt his body tense next to hers, and he pulled away. When he spoke again, there was a ragged edge to his voice.

"You want to leave?"

"I'm just talking."

"Are you serious?"

"You asked me, and I'm telling you."

She wanted to say more, but he wasn't listening.

"One year," he said. "We agreed we'd give this one year. Now, three months in and you're ready to pack up and run back to Chicago."

Megan didn't say anything.

"I thought things have been better," he said. "You made a friend, and you told me you've been getting out of the house more. I don't understand."

"Forget it," she said. "I take it back."

"Do you think it's that easy to take back?"

Megan closed her eyes. "What do you want me to say?"

"Nothing." Tyler rolled onto his side, his back to her. "You've said enough."

She expected him to say something else, but he didn't, and for a long time she stayed staring up at the night-blue ceiling, listening to his breathing.

Eventually, he was asleep.

Megan pushed the covers away, slipped out of bed, and headed downstairs to the kitchen. She took a cup from the cabinet and poured herself a glass of water from the tap.

She drank half of it and dumped the rest.

Her hands were shaking, and she squeezed them into fists before opening the cabinet above the refrigerator and taking down the bottle of bourbon. She poured three fingers into the empty glass and carried it, along with the bottle, into the living room.

She stood at the window, staring out at the shadow of Rachel's house on the corner, and listening to the sharp, creeping pulse of the grandfather clock.

Soon, her glass was empty.

When she reached for the bottle to pour another drink, she noticed her hands had stopped shaking.

14

M egan?"
Tyler's voice pulled at her.

When she opened her eyes, she was lying on the couch in the living room. Tyler was standing over her, dressed for work, his travel mug in hand.

She sat up slowly. "What time is it?"

"Early."

Megan leaned forward and rested her head in her hands. Her glass from the night before was sitting empty on the coffee table beside the bottle of bourbon.

Her head hurt.

"Thought you'd want to move to the bed."

She looked up at him, but the light from the windows burned her eyes and she turned away. "You're leaving?"

"It's that time," he said, starting for the door. "I'll call you this afternoon, and we'll talk."

"You don't have to do that."

Tyler laughed and took his keys from the bowl. "Why, did you have another change of heart?"

The sarcasm in his voice was thick, but she ignored it. "I don't want to talk about it anymore, that's all."

"If only it were that easy."

He walked out, and a minute later Megan heard his car back down the driveway. She sat for a while, listening to the pounding tick of the grandfather clock. Then she took the empty glass and the bourbon from the coffee table and carried them into the kitchen.

She put the bottle back in the cabinet above the refrigerator and rinsed the glass in the sink. She filled it with cold water and drank, finishing it in three large swallows. Immediately, she felt better. Not perfect, not even close, but the pain in her head faded a little, and she didn't feel like throwing up anymore.

She considered it a victory.

Setting the glass in the sink, she headed upstairs to the bedroom and crawled into bed. She took Tyler's pillow and put it over her head, blocking out all light and sound. She could smell him on the pillow, and the scent touched something inside of her, making her ache.

Within minutes, she was asleep.

———

Lost in a blue light.

———

It was almost noon when she woke up. Her headache was gone, but every muscle in her body was stiff and sore. She slid out of bed and into the shower. The heat helped clear her head, and she stayed under the water until it ran cold.

When she got out, she felt almost human.

Once she was dressed, she went downstairs to the kitchen. There was a sticky note on the coffeemaker.

Ready to go. Press start.

Despite their conversation the night before, Tyler still set up the coffee for her before he left for work. The gesture, both simple and sweet, made her smile. But when she reached out and pushed the button and heard the coffee start to brew, she felt nothing.

It scared her, and she didn't know what to do.

There was no clear path.

She wanted to leave Willow Ridge, but not without Tyler. She wanted to tell him about Rachel, how something was wrong with her, but she knew he wouldn't listen.

After a while, the coffeemaker beeped.

Megan grabbed her yellow cup from the dish drainer and filled it. She drank half of it while standing at the sink. Then she set the cup on the counter, headed for the front door, and took her shoes from the closet.

She needed to clear her mind.

Fiona was right, walking with her had helped, and even though she didn't want to go alone, she knew that getting out of the house would make it easier to think.

At least, it wouldn't make things worse.

———

Megan walked for a long time, and she was about to turn around and head home when she saw the rabbit.

It was lying on its side in the gutter, and it looked so perfect that at first she wasn't convinced it was dead. It hadn't been there for long. There was no blood, no insects, and no injuries that she could see.

Most likely, she thought, it'd been clipped by a car and thrown, or crawled, to the side of the road to die.

It looked so perfect.

Above her, a single white cloud passed in front of the sun, and everything fell into shadow. Megan looked around at the suddenly dull green lawns and the muted, mirrored rows of pastel houses.

Then back down at the rabbit.

As the cloud cleared the sun, the shadows faded away, and the sunlight shimmered off the rabbit's fur.

Megan bent down for a closer look.

Part of her almost expected the rabbit to get up and run away, slipping seamlessly back into the world.

But it didn't.

She stepped off the sidewalk and into the gutter and nudged the back of the rabbit with her toe. She wasn't sure what she was expecting, but when nothing happened, she did it again, harder.

Then she heard a man's voice behind her.

"My heart has joined the thousand, for my friend stopped running today."

Megan turned around, fast.

The man standing behind her was older. He had short gray hair and a ragged silver beard that touched the top of his chest. There were several faded green tattoos running up his arms and disappearing under the sleeves of his black T-shirt.

He smiled, his teeth perfect and white.

Instinctively, Megan stepped back.

"Sorry." He motioned to the rabbit in the gutter, his smile fading. "*Watership Down*. Seemed appropriate."

Megan put a hand to her chest, didn't speak.

"I really do apologize," he said. "I didn't mean to scare you like that."

"I just didn't hear you."

"It's the ghost in me." He laughed at his own joke and stepped closer, looking down at the rabbit. "Another fallen soldier in the great automobile wars, I see."

Megan followed his gaze. "Looks that way."

"Did you think kicking it would help, or do you have something against rabbits?"

"God, that makes me sound terrible."

The man winked at her, and even though her heart was beating hard, and she could still feel the cold rush of adrenaline running through her, a part of her liked him immediately, and she couldn't help but smile.

"I'm not crazy about squirrels myself." He shook his head. "So I understand the impulse."

She laughed even though it wasn't that funny. "Nothing like that. I was just making sure it was dead."

"You thought it was faking?"

"Hard to tell around here."

Megan didn't know why she said it, and she regretted the words right away, but it was too late. The man stared at her, hard, and for a second she thought she saw a flash of fear pass behind his eyes.

"Why do you say that?"

The air between them felt thick. Megan tried to backtrack, pretending she didn't notice the shift. "It looks like it's asleep, don't you think?"

The man watched her, silent.

"Did I say something wrong?" she asked.

The man seemed to snap back, but his eyes never left hers. She was about to say something else, but before she could, he leaned in and spoke softly.

"You've seen it, too?"

A sudden chill spread through her. She wanted to act like she didn't know what he was talking about, but she could tell he saw the truth on her face.

The old man's eyes went wide.

He whispered to himself, "Oh Christ."

Every muscle in Megan's body tightened, and when she spoke, her voice cracked.

"I'm sorry," she said. "I don't know what you're—"

The man put a finger to his lips and shook his head. The movement was subtle, but there was no mistaking it. His eyes moved past her toward the houses across the street, then back down to the rabbit in the gutter.

He didn't say anything else.

The feeling they were being watched was overwhelming, and Megan stepped closer. "What did you mean?"

There was a pause, then the old man turned and looked up at the blue sky, the sunlight revealing deep lines in his skin. He inhaled slowly, and Megan watched his shoulders rise and fall with his breath.

When he looked back at her again, his eyes were soft.

"You must think I'm crazy," he said. "I'm sorry about that. Sometimes I forget myself."

There was a new falseness to his voice that Megan wasn't expecting, but before she could say anything, he held out his hand and she surprised herself by taking it.

"David Mercer," he said. "Everyone calls me Mercer."

"Megan Stokes."

"It's a pleasure."

Mercer's hand was calloused, and when he let go, his skin made a rough scraping sound as it passed over hers.

"I've seen you before, walking with Fiona Matheson." He looked past her, scanning the street. "Is she with you today?"

"Not today," Megan said. "She's working."

"I see." He stepped back. "Well, it was a pleasure to meet you, Megan. Maybe I'll see you again."

"Wait," she said. "Can you tell me what you meant?"

"Meant about what?"

"You asked if I'd seen it, too." She paused. "What did you mean by that? Seen what?"

Mercer's eye twitched, and for a second the sharpness returned. Then it was gone, and his face stayed calm.

"It's my age," he said. "Sometimes I get confused. To hear my daughter talk about it, you'd think I—"

Megan's eyes narrowed.

Mercer noticed and smiled.

She waited for him to go on, but instead he stepped closer and leaned in.

"The sweepers come at night." He nodded toward the rabbit in the gutter. "By tomorrow it'll be gone."

He reached out and put a hand on her arm, squeezing a gentle good-bye. Then he turned and headed off down the sidewalk toward the houses at the end of the street.

Megan watched him walk away.

The sweepers come at night?

She tried to make sense of it, but it meant nothing to her, so she started following him. She wanted to ask him again what he meant, but before she could catch up, Mercer turned up the walkway toward a pale-green house at the end of the block.

By the time she got there, he was already inside, and the door was closed.

15

T yler brought Chinese food and a bottle of wine home for dinner. They sat together at the table and ate out of the boxes with wooden chopsticks. He told her about his day, and she told him about meeting Mercer on her walk.

"His name is Mercer?"

"David Mercer," she said. "He just goes by Mercer."

Tyler shrugged. "I think it's great you went without Fiona. I didn't think you would."

"I don't see why," she said. "I'm not a shut-in."

Tyler agreed and reached for the bottle of wine and refilled her glass. "Did it make you feel better?"

"No," she said. "Worse."

He set the bottle back on the table and leaned over his food, chopsticks picking through the box. Then he set them on the table and said, "Megs, I can't leave. You know that, right?"

Megan nodded. "Yeah, I know."

"Maybe in a year, but not now. Not yet."

She took one last bite, then pushed the box of lo mein away and reached for her glass. The wine was sweet and good, and she tried to focus on that and nothing else.

"I want you here with me," he said. "I need you here with me. If you give it a little more time, I know things will get better."

"How do you know?"

"I just do."

Megan set her glass on the table and absently ran her finger around the rim, silent.

"What do you think?" he asked.

She looked over at him, staring.

He frowned. "What's wrong?"

"I saw Rachel yesterday."

Tyler eased back in his chair, didn't speak.

"Have you seen her recently?" she asked.

"Not since you called me home to check on her."

There was an edge to the comment, but Megan ignored it.

"I saw her outside for the first time in days, so I went down there and—"

"Jesus, Megan."

"She didn't say anything to me," Megan said. "I'm not even sure she can speak."

"What the hell does that mean?"

"It means she's different."

"Different? How?"

Megan shook her head, then lifted her glass and took a drink. "I'll make you a deal, but I want you to do something for me."

She watched the suspicion build in his eyes.

"What do you want me to do?"

"I want you to go see her again. And I want to be there with you when you do."

"I don't understand," he said. "Why are you—"

"If you do this for me, if you see her, and if you think everything's completely normal, then I'll stay."

Tyler seemed to think about it. "You want to do this tonight?"

Megan glanced toward the window and the black sky beyond. She shook her head. "No, we'll go tomorrow. After you get home."

Tyler stared at her; the expression on his face sat somewhere between anger and desperation.

"Sometimes," he said, "I really don't understand you."

"I don't think it's asking too much," Megan said. "Tomorrow night. We'll go together."

"And if I do this, you'll—"

"I'll stay." She paused. "As long as you don't think anything is out of the ordinary."

Tyler nodded in agreement, and Megan felt some of the tension in the room fade. Then he reached for his glass and held it up, waiting for her to do the same. When she did, he touched his to hers and said, "Whatever makes you happy."

Megan smiled.

They both drank.

———

That night Megan couldn't sleep.

Her mind kept drifting toward tomorrow, wondering what Tyler would say, or how he'd react once he saw Rachel.

The uncertainty of it terrified her.

Every time she drifted close to sleep, all that came were blue dreams and a familiar, desperate emptiness that pulled her awake. So she lay there, staring up at the soft shifting shadows on the ceiling, until eventually she gave up trying to sleep and slipped out of bed.

Tyler didn't stir.

Megan walked downstairs to the kitchen and took the bottle of bourbon from the cabinet and poured a drink. This time, she left the bottle behind instead of taking it with her into the living room.

She'd learned her lesson.

Cradling the glass in her hands, she stood at the window and stared out at the dark and silent street. Once again, she thought about Rachel and wondered how Tyler was going to react when he saw what had happened to her.

She ran through several scenarios, none of them good,

and her thoughts spun with all the terrible possibilities.

When she finished her drink, she set the empty glass on the coffee table and curled up on the couch. It was comfortable, and she closed her eyes, losing herself in the steady ticking of the grandfather clock.

Then she heard a new sound.

Engines.

She opened her eyes and saw shadows pan across the blue room.

Megan pushed herself up and looked out the window. There were three white vans moving slowly down the street in front of her house. Their headlights were off, and their windows were a deep, empty black.

When they got to Rachel's house, the first van pulled into the driveway. The other two stopped along the street out front. All the doors swung open at once, and several men climbed out, dressed in black.

They moved with no hesitation.

It was like watching a machine.

The men split into groups. The first group circled around to the back of Rachel's house; the next climbed the porch steps and went inside through the front door. Several others stayed by the vans, unpacking large hard-shell cases that they stacked on top of each other before rolling them up the driveway toward the house.

The last four met in the intersection.

They stood together, face-to-face. Then they each took a

small device from their belts and split up, moving down different streets, away from the intersection.

Megan squinted against the darkness, but she couldn't see what they were carrying. As they moved out of the intersection, all four devices began to glow, sending out flat, cold beams of blue light that panned over the streets and the rows of quiet houses.

The sweepers come at night.

Megan wanted to hide.

She stepped back from the window, but then she saw a man come out of Rachel's house and stand on the porch. He pointed to the white van in the driveway, and one of the men opened the side door as two other men walked out of the house carrying what looked like a long black body bag between them.

The bag was heavy, and it sagged in the middle.

"Oh my God."

Megan's voice was a whisper, but her thoughts were screaming.

She's dead.

They found her, and she's dead.

Megan could feel herself start to spiral, and she ran through everything that would happen next. There would be an investigation, people would talk, the questions would start, and then they'd get to her.

And then—

She stopped.

The man she'd seen walking along her street was now

standing in front of her house, watching her, his face hidden by shadow. He was holding the glowing blue device in front of him, close enough for her to see it clearly.

It looked like a small glass pyramid.

Megan tried to step away from the window, but she couldn't move. She wanted to yell out, wanted to wake Tyler, but she had no voice.

Outside, the man lifted the pyramid, and the blue light passed over her. She felt a sudden rush of cold that sank into her skin, squeezing her, pulling at her.

Then it was gone, and there was only darkness.

16

When Megan woke up, she was lying on the couch. The sun was shining, but the light coming through the windows was wrong. Her glass from the night before was still on the coffee table, and there was a red cashmere blanket draped over her.

She sat up slowly, glanced at the grandfather clock.

It was almost six o'clock.

Megan stared at the clock for a long time, not believing what she was seeing. Then she leaned forward and rested her head in her hands, waiting for her thoughts to clear, and for everything to make sense.

I slept all day?

When she looked up again, she saw a note sitting on the table next to her glass. She picked it up and read:

Megan,
You fell asleep on the couch, and I couldn't
bring myself to wake you up. Coffee is ready to
go. See you tonight.
  Love,
  T.

Slowly, the fog began to lift, and the night before came back to her. Megan got up and hurried to the window and looked out at Rachel's house. Mr. Addison's Cadillac was in the driveway, and for the first time in days, all the curtains in the house were open. There were no police cars out front, no ambulances, and no white vans.

Only the Cadillac and the roses and the sunshine.

It was a dream.

The idea made sense, but as much as Megan wanted it to be true, she knew it wasn't. What she saw last night had been too vivid to be a dream, too real.

She stayed at the window, watching Rachel's house. She was about to turn away when the front door opened and Mr. Addison stepped outside. He stood on the porch for a moment, stretched, then walked down the steps and along the walkway toward his car in the driveway.

She watched him stop behind the car and flip through a set of keys. Then he unlocked the trunk and took out a heavy black suitcase. He closed the trunk, spun the keys on his finger, and headed back to the house.

There was such a casual joy in the way he walked that

Megan began to wonder if she'd been wrong. Maybe what she saw the night before had been a dream after all. And this time, she found it harder to convince herself that it wasn't.

Megan glanced at the clock again and frowned.

The day was gone, and Tyler would be home soon. He still thought they were going to see Rachel, but Megan was no longer sure what they'd find, and that was a problem.

Tyler needed to see her.

Megan turned away from the window and ran upstairs to get dressed. When she came back down, she slipped on her red Chuck Taylors and headed for Rachel's house.

———

Mr. Addison opened the front door as she came up the steps, as if he'd been waiting. When he saw her, his face lifted into a wide, slightly confused smile.

"Hello, Mrs. Stokes."

Megan stopped at the top of the steps. "Sorry to drop in on you like this. Is it a bad time?"

"Not at all, what can I do for you?"

Megan tried to look past him into the house, but he blocked her view, and all she could see were shadows.

"Mrs. Stokes?"

She looked at him, and his smile wavered.

"I'm sorry," she said. "I don't—"

"Is everything okay?" he asked. "You look a bit pale."

"I'm fine." She tried her best to smile. "I got lost there for a minute. I'm okay, really."

Mr. Addison watched her, and she could tell he didn't believe her, but he played along.

"Would you like to come inside? I can make some tea, or we have coffee if you'd rather—"

"Actually, I came by to talk to Rachel about the Ashland Renovation Project. I was thinking about taking part this year, and I wanted to ask her if—"

"They invited you?"

There was a hint of skepticism in his voice, but Megan didn't let it sway her.

"Not exactly," she said. "Fiona Matheson mentioned it, and I don't have much going on right now. I thought if I could be useful, I might as well help out."

Mr. Addison leaned against the doorframe, crossing his arms over his chest. His stomach was large, and it fell in a thick roll over his belt.

"They don't normally let new residents take part in the renovations."

"Why not?"

The question seemed to surprise him, but he recovered quickly. "I really don't know. That's something you should probably ask Fiona. I'm sure she'd be able to explain how it works better than I can."

"I'll ask her next time I see her," Megan said. "But since I'm here, is Rachel home? I might as well talk to someone who's done it in the past."

"I'm afraid you missed her," he said. "She left this morning to visit her sister in San Francisco."

"She's gone?"

"She'll be back in a few days," he said. "I'm sure she'll be happy to talk to you about the project, although she hasn't taken part in a while."

Megan stepped back from the door, then turned and glanced up the street toward her house. There was a dull buzz behind her eyes, and she could tell something was wrong. The sky seemed too bright, too far away, and the world felt like it was spinning around her.

For a second she was gone.

Then there was a hand on her arm, steadying her.

Mr. Addison was next to her, one hand on her elbow, the other on her shoulder. "Mrs. Stokes, are you okay?"

She nodded, but she didn't say anything.

"Why don't you come inside and sit for a while," he said. "Get out of the sun. Rest for a minute."

Megan shook her head, trying to clear it. Then she took her arm back and said, "Thank you, but I'll be okay."

"Please," he said. "I insist."

She started to argue, but then the muscles in her legs went weak. She reached for the railing, steadying herself, but at that moment she wasn't sure if she'd be able to make it home.

"Maybe a glass of water," she said. "You don't mind?"

"Of course not." He led her toward the door, motioning

her inside. "You can have a seat in the dining room. I'll bring it to you."

Megan thanked him, then stepped in and looked around.

When she'd seen the house through the window, it'd been destroyed, rooms torn apart, furniture broken and scattered. But now, everything looked perfect.

Immaculate.

"Would you like ice?"

His voice brought her back. "Yes, thank you."

Mr. Addison motioned to the dining room table. "Have a seat. I'll be right there."

Megan pulled a chair away from the table and sat down. She glanced around the room, searching for anything damaged or out of place.

There was nothing.

She thought about how the room looked when she'd seen it through the window, and again, she couldn't help but wonder if it'd all been in her head.

There was no other way to explain it.

And if she'd imagined what she saw inside the house, what else had she imagined?

Maybe Tyler had been right all along.

Behind her, she heard Mr. Addison dropping ice cubes into a glass before turning on the faucet. Megan closed her eyes and tried to slow her thoughts. She needed to get out, to go back and figure out what was happening before Tyler got home.

She pushed away from the table, and as she stood up, she noticed a shine on the wall next to the window. She moved closer and reached down, touching the spot.

Her fingers came away wet.

Fresh paint.

"Here you go." Mr. Addison came into the room with two glasses of ice water. He saw her fingers and looked past her toward the wall and frowned. "Is everything okay? How are you—"

Megan cut him off. "You know, I'm actually feeling better. I should probably head back. My husband will be home soon."

Mr. Addison watched her, silent.

"Thank you for letting me rest a minute," Megan said. "I think it helped."

The kindness in his face was gone, replaced by a look she didn't like. For a second, she was afraid of what he might do, but he just nodded and said, "I'll make sure to tell Rachel you stopped by."

"You don't have to do that."

"It's not a problem," he said. "I'm going to call her tonight and check on her anyway."

"Is she okay?"

"She's fine," he said. "At least she was before she left, but that was before seeing her sister. Now all bets are off. You know how it is with family."

"How has she been lately?" she asked. "You haven't noticed anything strange about her, or the way she's been—"

"What do you mean?"

His eyes turned sharp, and she stopped talking.

They were both quiet.

When he spoke again, the tone of his voice had changed, become hard, unwavering. "Rachel is fine, Mrs. Stokes. Are we clear on that?"

Megan felt a shiver start at the base of her spine and spread through her. "I'm sorry, I just—"

"I'll make sure she knows you stopped by."

She thanked him, and he led her out.

As she walked down the path toward the sidewalk, Megan could feel him staring at her, and when she reached the street, she crossed over quickly, moving toward her house.

Behind her, she heard his front door slam shut.

17

M egan took her coat from the closet and the car keys from the bowl by the door. Then she walked out to the garage and dropped her coat in the trunk next to the bag she'd left there a couple days earlier.

This time, she didn't think about whether she was making the right choice. She was beyond that. Something was happening in Willow Ridge, and all she knew was that she was completely alone.

Leaving was her only choice.

She shut the trunk and walked around to the driver's side and climbed in. Her hands were shaking, and it took a few tries to get the key into the ignition. Eventually, the key went in, and she started the engine.

She put the car in reverse, but she didn't back out.

Megan squeezed the steering wheel, trying to relax. She

knew that if she left, she wouldn't be coming back, but she also didn't see any other way.

With Rachel gone, Tyler would never believe her. If she kept pushing, things would only get worse between them, and sooner or later, they'd break.

And then it would be too late.

Her only option was to leave.

Megan checked her mirror and backed out of the garage. As she drove through the neighborhood toward the highway, she didn't look back once. She told herself that when she got to Chicago, she would call Tyler and try to explain. She would tell him she changed her mind, and that she just couldn't stay.

Maybe, she thought, he'd even forgive her.

———

County Road 11, between Willow Ridge and Ashland, cut a long two-lane scar through a seemingly endless stretch of shimmering green cornfields.

Megan drove fast.

Outside her window, the sun sat low on the horizon, turning the sky a depthless red, and casting long shadows over the road ahead.

When she'd first moved to Willow Ridge, she loved the drive into Ashland. There was a calm beauty to the land that she'd never seen before, and it'd surprised her. Now, when she looked out at the deep, rolling fields passing outside her window, all she saw was emptiness, isolation, and the endless passage of time.

But not for long.

Soon she'd be home.

She was still two miles outside Ashland when the rattle in the engine started again. The sound sent a chill through her that started in the center of her chest and spread down her arms and into her hands.

"Oh no," she whispered. "Please don't."

She listened for a while, hoping the rattle would stop. Then she looked out at the darkening sky and tried to decide what to do. She could keep driving, but I-80 was another twenty-five miles away, and by the time she made it that far, if she made it that far, it would be well into night.

Her only other option was Ashland.

She remembered seeing a gas station with a garage in town, and she thought she might be able to make it there. She hoped they could fix the engine on the spot, or better yet, tell her the rattle wasn't anything serious and she could keep going.

Megan wanted to believe that the noise wasn't serious, but she couldn't take the chance. She hadn't seen another car since leaving Willow Ridge, and the last thing she wanted was to break down at night on a deserted highway in the middle of nowhere.

She had to stop.

Up ahead she saw a familiar sun-faded sign on the side of the road showing a poorly drawn vanilla ice-cream cone.

The line under the cone said:

ASHLAND CREAMERY—1 MILE
HURRY IN BEFORE YOU MELT

Megan never understood that tagline, or why the Ashland Creamery would go with it for their sign. She felt a pang of annoyance over it, but then the engine made a loud cracking sound, and the car lurched around her.

The sign was forgotten.

The Corsica's steering wheel began to shudder, vibrating up her arms, and the rattle in the engine grew louder, like a handful of loose coins spinning in a dryer.

The air smelled like burning oil.

"Shit."

The idea occurred to her that she might end up stuck in Ashland, and for a second she considered turning around and trying to go back, but it was too late for that. Willow Ridge was miles behind her.

Ashland was her only choice.

As she got close to town, the speed limit changed from fifty-five to thirty. Megan slowed down and noticed dark smoke leaking out from under the hood. She glanced out at the silos and barns rising up along both sides of the road and said a silent prayer to anyone listening that she'd make it the rest of the way into town.

When she saw the sign for downtown Ashland, she turned

off CR-11, rumbled over a set of railroad tracks, and drove past several small wooden houses and tree-lined streets toward the center of town. The rattle in the engine shook the entire car, and Megan squeezed the steering wheel so tight that the muscles in her arms cramped.

Then the houses disappeared, replaced by two-story brick buildings on both sides of Main Street, each with storefronts below and smaller windows above.

The one streetlight in town, where First Avenue crossed Main, hung lifeless and forgotten over the intersection. Megan drove through, passing the market and the bank. The garage was a few blocks down, across from a public park filled with ash trees. She could just see the top of the station's A-frame roof, and as she got closer, a thought hit her, making her stomach drop.

What if it's closed?

She ignored the possibility, but the fear never left her. And when she pulled in next to the two gas pumps, that fear came rushing in and she couldn't fight it.

"No, no, no . . ."

Behind the pumps, the station's amber windows reflected the glow of the evening light. There was a piece of plywood nailed over the front door, and several rusted skeletons of old cars were parked along the side of the building next to a weatherworn two-port garage.

Megan stopped out front, feeling her stomach twist. She tried to think about what to do next, but the garage had been her only hope, and now it was gone.

She started to pull out of the lot, but then she saw movement behind the glass and felt a sharp glimmer of hope.

Someone was inside.

Megan pulled around and parked in front of the garage. When she shut off the engine, the car gave one final metallic shudder, and a rolling cloud of black smoke lifted into the air from the exhaust.

Then nothing.

Megan leaned back, exhaled slowly, and got out. The wind outside was strong and cold. She took her coat from the trunk and put it on as she moved across the lot toward the main building.

As she walked, she glanced over at the ash trees in the park across the street and watched them sway in the wind. She could hear the nervous rustle of their leaves. The sound was loud, like the chittering of insects.

When she reached the front of the building, a part of her was sure it would be locked. But then she pulled the handle, and the door swung open easily.

A delicate chime sounded above her head as she stepped inside.

The room was small, and the air smelled like grease and dust. There was a vending machine in one corner and a white pegboard along the far wall. Most of the hooks were empty except for a few plastic-wrapped air fresheners and a line of bungee cords.

At the back of the room was a glass-topped counter beside an open wooden door. A young boy in a faded Denver Broncos T-shirt stood behind it.

He stared at her.

Megan said, "Are you here by yourself?"

The kid looked at her, studying her face.

She gave him a minute, then tried again.

"Do you work here?"

The boy's eyes narrowed, and he leaned forward.

"Beep, beep, bop-bop." He tilted his head to one side and smiled, showing yellow teeth. "Bop-bop. Does not compute."

Megan frowned. "Is there someone else who—"

The boy turned slowly. "Boop, boop-bee deep."

A man's voice, deep and harsh, came from behind the open wooden door. "Travis, knock that shit off."

The boy stopped, smiled at her, shrugged.

Megan angled over to look past the open door, but before she could see anything, a man in a gray T-shirt stepped out, wiping his hands on a greasy red rag.

He saw her, then looked down at the boy and frowned.

"What the hell is wrong with you?" He put one large, grease-stained hand on the boy's shoulder and led him, not gently, off the stool toward the open door. "Go back and help your sister."

Once the boy was gone, the man dropped the rag on the far end of the counter and said, "Sorry about that." He tapped the side of his head with one finger. "That kid has never been quite right upstairs."

"It's okay," Megan said. "I understand."

The man nodded. "Was that you who pulled in?"

She told him it was.

"Sounds like you're having some trouble."

"Do you think you can help?"

"I think I can take a look," he said. "Can't promise I can help, but I'll see what I can do."

Megan felt a rush of relief, and it must've shown on her face because the man held up one hand. "Don't get your hopes up. It didn't sound too good."

"I know," she said. "But anything you can do."

The man grabbed the rag off the counter and slid it into his back pocket as he came around. Megan followed him to the door, but before they walked out, she heard giggling coming from the back of the room.

She turned in time to see two small heads duck back behind the open wooden door.

Megan frowned and walked out.

18

S he followed the man across the parking lot to her car. When they got there, he asked her to pop the hood.

She did.

The man braced it open with the prop. Then he stepped back, waving away heat and smoke.

"Try to start it."

Megan slid the key into the ignition and turned it. The engine made a short, cracking sound.

"Okay, that's enough."

She got out and walked around to the front of the car. "It's been making a noise for a while. What do you think?"

The man took the red rag from his pocket, leaned over the engine and reached in, wiping away dirt and oil. He didn't say anything at first. Then he frowned and stepped back. "Do you have another way home?"

The tone of his voice was resigned, and a dull weight settled in the pit of her stomach.

"This car, I hope."

"'Fraid not," he said. "How about someone you can call? Is there anyone who can pick you up and take you back to the Ridge?"

"How do you know I'm from Willow Ridge?"

The man looked at her for a long moment, and Megan saw a smile in his eyes. "Lucky guess?"

She decided to let it go.

"I'm not going back there," she said. "I'm on my way to Chicago."

"By yourself?"

Megan frowned. "You see anyone else in the car?"

The second the words were out, she regretted them. This man was her only chance of getting her car fixed, and the last thing she needed to do was start a fight with him over a woman's ability to drive across the country alone.

If it meant getting her car fixed and getting back on the road, she was willing to put up with almost anything, even small-minded, small-town opinions.

Except, he didn't seem to care.

"Hate to tell you, but this car isn't going to Chicago. It's not even going back to the Ridge unless you know someone with a tow truck."

"You can't fix it?"

"Not a chance," he said. "The engine's seized."

"And that's bad?"

He nodded. "Yeah, that's bad."

Megan folded her arms over her chest and looked out at the park across the street, the ash trees swaying in the distance.

She wasn't ready to give up.

"How about a bus?"

"A what?"

"A bus," she said. "Is there a bus station in town? Can I buy a ticket to Chicago?"

He shook his head. "There are no buses."

"There has to be something," she said. "How do people get anywhere around here?"

The man slipped the rag back into his pocket. Then he reached up, closed the hood, and motioned toward the garage. "If you'd like, you can use the phone to call for a ride. Best I can do."

"What about the car?"

"We can push it around back, maybe salvage it for parts." He looked down at it, resting his hands on his hips. "Nothing else I can do."

"Parts?" She laughed, even though it wasn't funny. "It can't be that bad. What about a new engine, or replacing what's broken? Can't you order whatever it is you need to fix it?"

He shook his head. "Miss, this is an old car. It's seen its last days. I'm sorry."

Megan looked down at the Corsica, paused. "I've had it since college. It's the first thing I ever bought myself."

The man watched her, his eyes kind.

"Come on inside," he said, starting for the garage. "You can use the phone, call for a ride."

Megan leaned against the car as he walked away. After a few steps, he realized she wasn't behind him, and he stopped and looked back.

"Do you want to think about it?"

She nodded.

"Take your time," he said. "Every place around here closes up at about nine, but I'll be open until eleven. After that, you're on your own."

"I understand."

He stared at her, a deep line forming between his eyebrows, as if debating something.

"You really don't want to go back there, do you?"

Megan smiled. "Doesn't look like I have a choice."

For a minute, she thought he was going to say something else, but he didn't. Instead, he just nodded, turned, and headed for the dark, A-frame building, and the boarded-up door.

Megan looked over at the park across the street. The sky was nearly dark, and the moon was already out, full and bright, turning everything a peaceful blue.

She thought about Tyler, and about what she was going to tell him when she called home. He would want to know why she went to Ashland, and she knew it wouldn't matter what she told him. He'd know she was trying to leave. And now, with no car, and no way to get to Chicago, she'd have no choice but to go back and settle in at Willow Ridge.

No matter how she looked at it, or how many different options she tried to imagine, in the end it was clear.

She was trapped.

———

Megan was in no hurry to go home, so instead of calling Tyler, she walked down to the road and glanced up at the hardware store on the corner. There was a diner a few doors farther down, and a laundromat beyond that.

She started walking.

Most of the buildings she passed were older and made of stone or brick. Each one had a large storefront window that faced out toward the sidewalk, and several of those windows were broken and boarded up.

It made her think of Fiona and her renovation project.

A few of the stores were open, but she didn't go inside. Instead, she stood on the sidewalk and watched the locals move between them. She didn't think she looked too out of place, but she could feel that all eyes were on her.

After a while, Megan got tired of the attention, and she headed back to the park across from the garage and sat on one of the benches next to a grass-covered knoll. There was a paved walking trail running through the center of the park. It was dotted with a string of antique street lamps, each one casting a small amber island of light along the path.

Megan could hear the wind passing through the trees around her, and when she looked up through the branches, her breath caught in her throat. The sky was an explosion of stars, more than she'd ever seen.

When she was younger, someone, she couldn't remember who, told her that nearly all the stars in the sky died out ages ago, and that their light was just now reaching the earth. So when people stared up at the night sky, what they were really doing was looking into the past and seeing how things once were.

Megan thought about that for a while, trying to remember who'd told her about the stars, but the memory was lost to time, and something inside of her began to ache.

In the distance, a dog barked.

She glanced back at the road. It was completely dark now, but the gas station lights were still on. She could see the shadow of her car parked where she'd left it next to the garage, and she understood that it was time to go.

Still, it took her a while to stand up.

As she walked back to the gas station, she told herself what a part of her had known ever since that night in Rachel's garage.

She was on her own.

From now on, she wasn't going to say anything about moving back to Chicago. She wouldn't talk to Tyler about Rachel, and she wouldn't tell him about the men she saw in the white vans. She wasn't going to mention her conversation with Mr. Addison, or how the damage she'd seen in their home had been fixed overnight.

From now on, she would keep everything to herself.

From now on, she was on her own.

19

S he made the call, but not to Tyler.

Thirty minutes later, Fiona pulled up outside the gas station in a white SUV. Megan was waiting outside, leaning against the hood of her car. She had her bag from the trunk sitting next to her on the ground, and when she opened the passenger door of the SUV and climbed in, Fiona looked at the bag with one eyebrow raised.

"So you *were* leaving."

"What?"

She nodded toward the bag. "Your getaway bag?"

"This is everything from my car," Megan said, dodging the question. "I can't believe it finally died."

Fiona stared at her, and Megan could tell that she wanted to say more. But she didn't. Instead, she turned the SUV around and pulled out of the parking lot and back onto the road and didn't say anything.

Megan let the silence build.

"Is this your car?"

"Institute's," Fiona said. "I don't get to use it too often, but they let me keep it just in case. Most of the time it's in the garage gathering dust."

"I'm glad you had it. I owe you."

"I don't mind."

Again, silence.

Main Street slipped by outside the window. Then it was gone. They passed the tree-lined streets and wooden houses, and they drove over the railroad tracks. Then Fiona turned onto CR-11, heading back to Willow Ridge.

"Are you wondering why I didn't call Tyler?"

"Not really."

"Is that true?"

Fiona glanced over at her, the light from the dashboard shining red against her face. "Megan, I know an escape bag when I see one." She paused. "Besides, Tyler called looking for you tonight. He said you two had plans to visit the Addisons, but you didn't show up."

Megan cringed. "Shit, I'm sorry."

"He wanted to know if you'd said anything about going back to Chicago," Fiona said. "He was worried."

"I didn't think he'd call you."

"I take it you two are having problems?"

"You could say that." Megan hesitated. "What else did he tell you?"

"He told me you asked him to move back with you, but that he wasn't ready to leave."

"That's all?"

"He said you promised him you'd stay if he went with you to see Rachel."

Megan turned toward the passenger window and looked out at the dark blur of cornfields passing outside.

"That got me thinking about the day I ran into you outside her house," Fiona said. "The day you—"

"Yeah, I remember."

Fiona hesitated. "Is there a problem between you and Rachel?"

"She's gone," Megan said. "She left town."

"That doesn't answer my—"

"She went to visit her sister," Megan said, cutting her off. "At least that's what her husband said."

"You don't believe him?"

"I don't know what to believe."

A minute passed, and then Fiona pulled over, slowing down and stopping along the side of the empty road. She put the car in park and turned in her seat.

"Tell me what's going on."

Megan looked up at her.

She wanted to tell her the truth, starting with the night in the garage, and ending with the white vans and seeing them take Rachel out of her house in a body bag. She wanted to confess, mostly because she didn't want to be alone anymore.

"I'm worried about you," Fiona said. "I thought we were friends."

"We are friends."

"Then let me help."

Megan shook her head. "You'll think I'm crazy. Tyler doesn't believe me. You won't believe me, either."

"You might be surprised."

Outside, the cornfields swayed black in the wind, chattering together under a swirling sea of dead stars.

Megan listened to the sound, trying to decide.

Eventually, she turned and faced Fiona. "I don't know where to start."

Fiona put her hand on Megan's arm. "Start with Rachel," she said. "Tell me what happened. Why were you outside her house that day?"

Megan shook her head and tried to tell her that she didn't want to start there, but when she looked up, Fiona was watching her, smiling, and she lost the words.

Megan took a deep breath and tried again.

This time, she told her everything.

———

Once Megan finished, Fiona sat back in her seat and stared out at the road, silent. A minute passed, then she reached down and put the SUV in gear and continued on toward Willow Ridge.

Megan let the silence drag on for a long time, but eventually she couldn't take it anymore.

"You don't believe me."

"I didn't say that."

"You didn't say anything."

"I just need a minute."

Megan gave her one.

"I'm not crazy."

"I never said you were."

"Everything I told you happened," she said. "I didn't imagine it. I know what I saw."

Fiona nodded, but she still didn't speak.

Megan could feel the fear and frustration building inside her, and all the muscles in her body twisted like they were about to snap. She wanted to tell Fiona to forget she said anything, and to drop her off at home and she'd never hear from her again.

But then Fiona spoke.

"When did Roger say she was coming home?"

"Who?"

"Rachel's husband." She glanced at Megan, her eyes reflecting the red from the dashboard. "He told you she was visiting her sister."

"That's what he said, but—"

"But you don't believe him."

Megan thought about her answer, shook her head. "I saw them carry her body out of the house."

"You saw a bag."

"A body bag."

"How do you know it was her?"

"Who the hell else would it be?" Megan's voice was harsh, and she held up one hand. "I'm sorry, I don't—"

"It's okay," Fiona said. "I'm trying to keep an open mind and make sense of all this, but it's not easy."

"I know."

Fiona didn't say anything for a minute. Then she nodded and said, "I believe you saw something."

Megan laughed, even though she didn't think it was funny. "Well, that's a start. It's more than I got from Tyler."

"You have to admit, it's a hell of a story."

Megan didn't speak.

"When did Roger say she'd be home?"

"A few days."

"He didn't say what day?"

"Why does that matter?"

"I want to talk to her when she gets back," Fiona said. "Right away. I don't want to wait."

Megan looked over at her, frowning. "Why would you talk to her?"

"Because I believe you," she said. "I believe that something happened to Rachel, and that you saw it. There could be a lot of explanations, but if she's up and walking around and taking vacations to visit family, I think we can rule out that she died, don't you?"

Fiona's voice was so reasonable, so calm, that Megan almost agreed with her. But then she thought about Rachel twitching and suffocating on the floor of her garage, and she couldn't.

"I know what I saw."

"Megan." Fiona's voice was patient. "If it *was* something else—if she knocked herself unconscious, or if she has some kind of brain injury—we need to help her. You agree with me on that, right?"

"She wasn't unconscious."

"I know you think that, but—"

"I don't think it, I know it."

Fiona sighed. "I want to see her so we can rule out every other possibility. Once we do that, then maybe I'll be willing to make the jump to zombie, but not before."

Megan couldn't help but smile. "Zombie?"

Fiona smiled back. "And here I was, thinking I'd seen it all around here."

20

They pulled off CR-11 and into Willow Ridge. Fiona hadn't said anything in a while, and Megan didn't push. The night seemed fragile, and while she didn't regret telling her, she wanted to let Fiona put it all together in her head for herself.

They were still a few blocks from Megan's house when Fiona stopped at an intersection and said, "I don't think you should say anything about this to Tyler."

"You mean about Rachel?"

"It's not my place, but he was upset when he called looking for you," she said. "I don't think there's any reason to make things worse between you two, especially since we don't know what's going on."

She'd already decided not to talk to Tyler about Rachel, but part of her didn't feel good about that choice. Having Fiona back up her decision made her feel better.

"Thank you," Megan said. "For believing me."

Fiona touched her arm, smiled. "Once Rachel gets back, we'll get all of this settled, I promise. Focus on fixing things with Tyler, and don't worry about any of this."

Megan nodded, but she knew there would be no way she could stop thinking about Rachel. Until it was resolved, it was going to be all she thought about, but she didn't say that to her. Fiona was only trying to help.

Instead, she told her she'd try.

Fiona turned back to the road and drove the last few blocks to Megan's house. The lights inside were on, and when she pulled into the driveway, the front door opened and Tyler stepped out.

Megan sighed. "Well, here we go."

"Good luck." Fiona leaned over and hugged her, and when she pulled back, she looked Megan in the eye and said, "If you need anything at all, you call me."

Megan opened the door and got out.

She crossed the lawn toward Tyler, who was watching from the porch, and stopped at the bottom of the stairs. She looked up at him, and neither of them said anything.

After a moment, he turned and went back inside.

Megan glanced over her shoulder and watched Fiona pull out of the driveway. Then she climbed the steps and walked through the open door and into the house.

———

"There's no way to fix it?"

"He told me we could sell it for parts."

Tyler made a dismissive sound and got up from the table. He took his plate to the kitchen and set it in the sink. "I want a second opinion. It doesn't sound like this guy knows what he's talking about."

"We couldn't get it to start at all," Megan said. "It didn't even turn over."

"That could be a lot of things."

"He said the engine was seized."

Tyler paused. "I'd still like to have someone else look at it."

"We'll have to get it towed."

"And that's just great." He turned and leaned against the counter. "I still don't understand why you drove it to Ashland. You knew that car needed work."

"I told you why," she said. "I wanted—"

"A change of scenery. Yeah, I got that part."

"What else do you want me to tell you?"

He looked at her for a long time. "When I came home and you weren't here, I thought you'd left for good."

Megan shook her head. "It wasn't for good."

Something in Tyler's eyes changed, and she could tell he knew the truth. Part of her expected him to get angry, to ask her why she wanted to leave. If he did, she didn't think she could lie.

But instead, he changed the subject.

"I ran into Roger Addison," he said. "Rachel is out of town for a few days."

"Visiting her sister."

Tyler nodded. "He mentioned you stopped by, told me you wanted to see Rachel."

There was a question behind the statement, but it wasn't one she wanted to answer, so she sidestepped it.

"I don't want to talk about her anymore," Megan said. "I don't even want to think about her. I want it to be like she doesn't even exist."

"Last night you wanted to go see her."

"That was a mistake."

"You had to have a reason."

"Not a good one," she said. "I don't want to think about Rachel Addison anymore."

"But I don't—"

"Tyler, let it go."

Thankfully, he did.

———

That night Tyler slept closer to her than he had in weeks, his arm around her waist, his body tight against hers. Normally, Megan would've liked to have him close, but this time there was something uncomfortable about it.

She didn't push him away or say anything, and she'd almost drifted off to sleep when she felt him kiss the back of her neck, soft, and press against her, not soft.

Megan pretended to be asleep.

Tyler put his hand on her shoulder, gently pulling her toward him. She resisted at first, but then gave in and let him roll her onto her back. Then he climbed on top of her, moving her legs apart.

Megan closed her eyes and waited.

When he finished, he rolled off and onto his side, his back to her, and fell asleep. Megan stayed in bed, staring up at the shadows on the ceiling. Then she got up and went into the bathroom. When she came back, she stood at the bedroom window and looked out at the empty street.

It was late.

She thought about the white vans she'd seen outside Rachel's house. Then she thought about Mercer and the dead rabbit and what he'd said to her.

The sweepers come at night.

Tomorrow, she decided, she would start asking questions. She would talk to the neighbors and see if anyone else noticed anything strange the night before. Fiona wanted her to wait until they had a chance to talk to Rachel, but she was done waiting.

Tomorrow, she would look for answers.

And she'd start with David Mercer.

Megan stood at the window for a while longer, thinking of all the things she wanted to ask Mercer, and when she finally climbed back into bed, she fell asleep almost at once.

And she dreamed . . .

———

. . . of music.

There are dark shapes everywhere, and the air around her is cool and sweet. She can hear voices, soft at first, growing louder.

Behind them, whistles and bells and the breathy wheeze of calliope music.

A carnival.

Megan feels someone take her hand, a child, pulling her along through the darkness. She looks down and sees the back of her head, her dark hair flowing out behind her as she runs, leading them both through the crowd of shadows.

Every step they take, the darkness fades.

Megan sees game booths, a carousel, and rows of barkers. In the distance, a blue Ferris wheel turning slowly over it all.

And everywhere she looks, there are people.

She hears them talking and laughing, but they don't move. Only their eyes follow as they weave among them, ducking and running through a blur of flashing lights and sound and the quiet spaces in between.

"Where are we going?"

The little girl holding her hand doesn't answer, and she doesn't look back. Up ahead, the Ferris wheel spins, its blue light shining out, covering them as they run.

Megan stares at it, unable to look away.

Lost in the light.

Then she feels the little girl's hand slip from hers, and when she looks down, the child is gone. All around, the people start to move, ignoring her, their voices loud.

Megan turns and scans the shifting crowd, searching for the girl, but she doesn't see her. Then the crowd breaks against her, pushing her farther along the path, toward the rolling blue light of the Ferris wheel.

Megan yells, "Where are you?"

But there is no answer, only the chatter of the crowd, the fading whirl of the bells, and the gentle rise and fall of the calliope music.

21

M egan woke up early the next morning, but it was almost noon by the time she left the house. Outside, the air was cool and smelled like freshly cut grass. She could hear an angry chorus of blue jays in the trees as she crossed the lawn toward the sidewalk, but when she looked up, she didn't see a single bird.

Next door, Edna Davidson was in her yard, moving an oscillating sprinkler from one spot to another. She was wearing a black silk robe with yellow flowers embroidered across the bottom and along the cuffs of the sleeves. Edna glanced up at Megan when she passed by, but when Megan waved, she turned away and went inside.

Megan frowned and kept walking.

As she made her way through the neighborhood, she noticed how quiet the streets seemed. Most of the people were at work during the day, but the longer she walked, the more she started to wonder. The few faces she did see watched her from behind windows as she passed by, or they turned away, ignoring her completely.

By the time she made it to Mercer's house, the feeling that something was wrong sat heavy in her mind. She did her best to push it away, but it wasn't until she started up the driveway and saw him in the garage, leaning over the engine of an old car, that the uneasiness faded, replaced by genuine curiosity.

The car was decades old, lemon yellow, with sharp fins and a white stripe along the side that widened toward the back. Mercer didn't see her until she was only a few feet away. Once he did, he stood up and stepped away from the car, socket wrench in hand.

"Don't tell me," he said, squinting. "Megan, right?"

"That's right." She smiled. "Good memory."

"For some things," he said. "Others, not so much."

"I hope you don't mind me stopping by."

"Not at all. Have you found any more rabbits?"

His voice sounded fun, but Megan noticed the way his eyes moved past her as he spoke, scanning the street and the houses around them.

She decided to get to the point.

"That's kind of why I'm here," she said. "I was hoping I could ask you a couple questions, if you don't mind."

"About the rabbit?"

"About a few things, actually."

"Sounds serious." He held up both hands. "I didn't kill that rabbit, I promise."

"I believe you."

"Good." He turned back to the lemon-yellow car and studied the engine as he spoke. "Happy to have that out of the way. So, what is it then?"

"You said something the other day, but you walked away before I could ask you about it."

Mercer looked up at her, his eyes sharp. He motioned to the toolbox on the ground by her feet. "Do me a favor. There's a flat-head screwdriver in there somewhere. A big one with a clear yellow handle. Grab it for me?"

Megan bent down and lifted the top tray from the toolbox. She found the screwdriver at the bottom and handed it to him.

"Thanks." He took the screwdriver and bent back over the engine. "Do you like old cars?"

Megan immediately thought about her Corsica sitting outside the gas station in Ashland, even though she knew that wasn't what he meant. The Corsica was old to her, but his car was at least thirty more years back.

"I like the design," she said. "What is it?"

"She." He paused, finished the adjustment he was making, and stepped back, wiping his hands on his shirt. "Cars are always female."

"I guess I knew that."

Mercer motioned to the car with the screwdriver and said, "She is a convertible 1957 Chevy Bel Air. I've been tinkering with her forever, but it seems like there's always something else that needs to be fixed."

"I'm sorry to hear that."

"Don't be," he said. "Who knows what I'll do with myself the day I finish with her."

"Go for a ride?"

Mercer glanced down at the car and smiled a thin, wistful smile. "Trouble is you can only go so far before you have to come back and find something else to do to pass the time. Which is probably why I'm still at it. Fear of letting her go."

Megan thought about this, and for a while they were both quiet. Then she said, "What are the sweepers?"

Mercer looked up at her, his smile gone.

"You mentioned them the other day when we saw that rabbit in the gutter," Megan said. "You told me the sweepers come at night. What did you mean?"

"Is that what you wanted to ask me?" The smile was back, but this time it didn't touch his eyes. "You want to know about the street sweepers?"

"That's what you were talking about?"

"Of course," he said. "They come through here at night when everyone is asleep, probably so they don't bother folks during the day."

Something in his voice was different, and when he slid past her and dropped the screwdriver back in the toolbox, Megan could feel the tension radiating off him.

"That's considerate of them to work at night."

Mercer nodded and went around to the front of the car and closed the hood. "The Institute takes care of their own around here, don't they?"

"Sure seems that way."

Megan watched him kneel next to the toolbox again and fasten the latches. Then he carried it across the garage and set it on the floor in the corner. When he turned back to her, he put his hands on his hips and shrugged.

"I think I need a shower," he said. "It was good of you to stop by. I hope you decide to do it again."

"Right." She lifted her hand, nodded. "I'll get out of your hair. Maybe next time I stop by, you'll be finished with her and you can take me for a ride."

Mercer winked. "Not if I can help it."

"That's right. Never let go."

"Not until they make you," he said. "And maybe not even then."

He started to walk away, but Megan stopped him.

"Mr. Mercer?"

He turned. "Just Mercer."

"Mercer," she said. "What did you mean when you asked if I'd seen it, too?"

He looked around at the street and the houses and the trees before coming back to her again. "Like I said, I'm an old man. Sometimes my thoughts get away from me. Half the time I don't know what I'm saying."

"I don't believe you."

Megan's voice was steady, matter-of-fact.

This time, when he looked at her, there was something new in his eyes. It wasn't humor and it wasn't anger.

It was fear.

"Look, I—"

"Because I have," Megan said. "I've seen things, and I think you have, too."

Again, Mercer's eyes moved past her, scanning the streets. "It's best to not talk about this."

"If you're trying to get rid of me, I'm not—"

"It's not that," he said. "Not entirely."

"Then what is it?" she asked. "What did you mean when you asked me that? What exactly is happening around here?"

"We can't discuss this," he said. "Not now."

Megan looked around, lifted her hands and let them fall. "Seems like a good time to me."

"It's not."

"Tell me why?"

"Megan—"

"Tell me."

Mercer hesitated, then leaned in, his voice barely above a whisper.

"Because they're watching."

22

Mercer took her arm and led her down the driveway. "I'll walk with you," he said. "Do you mind?"

Megan glanced around at the other houses along the street, but she didn't see anyone outside or standing in the windows. If someone was watching them, they were well hidden. Still, Mercer was obviously scared of something, so she kept quiet as they moved along the sidewalk.

As they walked, Mercer pointed out houses and told her a little about the people living inside, who they were, and how they were connected to the Institute. It was difficult to focus on what he was saying. She had so many questions that it took all of her willpower to keep them inside.

Megan tried to play along.

"What do you do at the Institute?"

"Nothing," he said. "I've never even been inside."

"Then why are you here?" she asked. "I thought you had to

work on the ridge to live here."

"My wife worked there." He smiled at the memory. "Brilliant woman. Here I am, barely able to calculate a tip at a restaurant, while she . . ."

His voice trailed away, and he was quiet for a long time. Eventually, she asked if he was okay, and he nodded.

"The woman intimidated me," he said. "So damn smart, even when we met as undergraduates. Part of me always found it baffling that we had anything to talk about at all. But we did. A lifetime's worth of things, as it turned out."

Again, Mercer went quiet, and Megan let the silence hang between them. Up ahead, the sidewalk curved to the south, and she could see the willow forest running along the base of the ridge. As they got closer, she could hear the whisper of the wind in the trees.

"How about you?" Megan asked. "What did you do?"

"Nothing, once we came here," he said. "At one time, I wrote novels, which meant I was somewhat of a bum."

"Were you published?"

"A few times."

"Then you weren't a bum," she said. "Sounds to me like you had some success."

"For whatever that's worth." He paused. "To be honest, I barely remember the days before we moved here. In a lot of ways, it was a different life."

"You quit writing when you moved here?"

"I found I didn't have the heart for it anymore, and thanks

to Anna's job, we didn't need the money." He leaned closer as they walked. "Do you know the secret to making a living as a novelist?"

Megan told him she didn't.

"Marry rich."

He laughed, and the sound was so joyful that she didn't have the heart to tell him it was an old joke. Instead, she laughed along with him and told him that was true for all artists.

"No doubt," he said, nodding. "No doubt."

They walked a little farther, and Megan could feel the pressure building inside of her with each step. She was starting to lose patience, and even though she didn't want to say anything, she couldn't hold back.

The words were out before she could stop them.

"When did you first notice strange things happening around here?"

Megan felt Mercer tense up, but he didn't say anything. She started to ask him again, but before she could, he lifted his hand and pointed to a pale-blue house halfway down the block.

"The man who owned that house was a friend of mine. His name was Tom Alexander. We both loved old cars. He moved on several years ago, but he was probably the first real friend I made around here."

The frustration was building, and Megan couldn't take it anymore. She stopped walking. Mercer took a few more steps, noticed she wasn't with him, and turned around.

"I need to know I'm not crazy," she said.

"How am I supposed to know that?"

"Tell me I'm not the only one."

Mercer hesitated, then he pointed toward the same pale-blue house halfway down the block and said, "Tom had an old hydraulic jack that he'd use when he had to work under a car. One afternoon he was fixing the transmission on a green 1969 Mustang when—"

"Mercer." Megan held up her hands. "Please, no more stories. Tell me what the hell is going on around—"

"When the car slipped off the jack."

Megan stopped talking.

He sighed, stepped closer. "I've made things worse for you. I never should've spoken to you that day, but when I saw you out there looking at that rabbit, I knew."

"You knew what?" she asked.

"That you'd seen it, too."

"Seen what?"

"How things around here move under the surface." He held up one finger. "And before you ask, I don't know much. I have theories, but no proof of anything."

"But something is happening here. I'm not crazy."

"No," he said. "You're not crazy."

The relief Megan felt was so strong that she wanted to cry, but she didn't. Instead, she focused on her breath and tried to keep her voice from cracking when she spoke.

"Tell me what you know."

Mercer looked down at her, and she could see the debate going on behind his eyes.

"Before she died, my wife told me about some of the experiments they were doing," he said. "I don't know how many people they study around here. I've known of at least seven personally, but I'm sure there are others."

"They?"

"The Institute," he said. "She showed me internal documents, diagrams I barely understood, and she tried to explain what they'd done and why they did it." He paused. "She was carrying a lot of guilt when she died."

"Guilt over what?"

"Over what they did to me, I assume."

"I don't understand. What did they—"

"How much do you know about what happens on the ridge?" he asked. "Has your husband told you about his job? Do you know what he does?"

"He's a systems technician."

"Technical or biological?"

Megan hesitated. "Technical."

Mercer's shoulders sagged. He stood there for a moment, looking around at the houses and the trees. Then he motioned for her to follow. She did, and they continued down the sidewalk toward the forest.

"Most of the documents my wife brought home were lost in the cleanse, but I was able to hide a few."

"The cleanse?"

"They sent a team to my house after she died, and they went through everything, quietly removing anything specific to the Institute." He paused. "They were thorough, but not thorough enough. I managed to hide a few things, but nothing more than random puzzle pieces."

"The white vans?"

Mercer stopped walking. "How do you . . . ?" He shook his head and waved the question away. "Never mind, I don't want to know."

"Are those the sweepers you told me about?"

"I don't know what they are," he said. "I only saw them once, after Anna died. I've always thought they were part of a dream. You're the first person I've met who knew about them."

"I saw them," she said. "They were—"

This time, when he held up a hand, she saw that it was shaking.

Megan decided to let it go. "What did your wife tell you?"

"She told me why I was here, why she couldn't let me go. She tried to explain the types of experiments they were running and what kinds of things they were working on." He went quiet for a moment, then said, "You asked me when I first noticed strange things happening around here."

She nodded.

"The day I woke up here," he said. "That was the first time."

"I don't understand."

Mercer stepped closer, pushed his sleeves up, and held out his arms.

There were two thin scars, like long pink worms, dug into his skin. The lines sliced across the inside of his wrists and ran from his palms up toward his elbows.

It took Megan a minute to understand what she was seeing. Once she did, she stared up at him, silent.

Mercer's eyes were clear and blue and focused on hers.

"I shouldn't be here," he said. "Yet here I am."

23

I don't remember much," Mercer said. "It wasn't as dramatic as a shotgun or swallowing a bottle of sleeping pills and then hiding in the crawl space under the house, but I'm sure it wasn't a cry for help, either."

Megan listened as he spoke, trying to stay focused. Her face and hands were numb, and her stomach ached, and as much as she wanted to hear what Mercer was saying, all she could think was she'd been right.

She wasn't crazy.

"That one didn't work, you know," Mercer said.

Megan barely heard him. "What?"

"The sleeping pills in the crawl space. That was Sylvia Plath who did that, but they found her. She got it right eventually: head in the oven—no muss, no fuss."

"Jesus."

Mercer stopped walking next to a low-cut stretch of grass

that ran between the sidewalk and the forest. To her left, Megan saw the last row of houses marking the far edge of Willow Ridge. She could just make out the top of Fiona's house in line with the others, and she wondered what Fiona would think of Mercer's suicide story.

"I apologize if I sound callous," he said. "But that's exactly what I am."

"I still don't understand," Megan said. "What you're telling me, it sounds impossible."

"Is what you've seen so much easier to believe?"

The thought stopped her.

He was right. Everything she'd seen fit with what he was telling her, and even though a part of her still didn't want to believe it, she knew he was telling the truth.

"You're saying the Institute is bringing people back to life?"

Mercer seemed to think about his answer. Then he nodded, and when he spoke, his voice sounded resigned.

"I suppose I am," he said. "Although my wife would've used the terms *neuro-reanimation* and *neuro-regeneration*."

"That can't be possible, can it?"

"I assure you, it is," he said. "And that's just the tip of what they're doing. I've seen several experiment reports. Documents listing the different techniques they're developing at the Institute and testing on people living right here in Willow Ridge."

Megan kept quiet, not sure what to say.

She realized her thoughts must've shown on her face, because Mercer nodded and said, "I know how it sounds. You think I'm out of my head, that I've lost my mind."

"I didn't say that."

"I haven't asked you what you've seen," he said. "Mainly because I already have an idea, but also because I don't want to know. I'll leave you to decide if what I've told you fits with your experiences here."

Megan kept quiet.

Mercer frowned, gestured toward the forest. "Do you see the electrical box next to the trees?"

Megan glanced over and nodded.

"If you walk straight past it, about twenty yards, you'll find a path leading to the creek. About a hundred yards in there's a wooden shed. I've hidden every one of the documents I was able to save inside a lockbox in that shed. I'd like you to see them, read them for yourself, and then you can decide if I'm crazy or not."

"Right now?"

Mercer looked up, squinting at the blue sky. Then he shook his head. "No, not now. It's too early, and there are too many eyes. We'll go tomorrow night after dark."

The thought of going into the forest after dark with a strange man didn't sit well, no matter what the reason, and she was trying to figure out what to say when she heard someone call her name.

Megan leaned to look past Mercer and saw Fiona coming down the sidewalk toward them, waving, her wooden clipboard cradled against her chest.

When Mercer saw her, he turned back to Megan.

"Let me show you what I have before you tell anyone else," he said. "Can I trust you to keep this between us?"

"I won't say anything."

He nodded, but Megan saw a flash of doubt in his eyes. Then, when Fiona came closer, he faced her, bright and smiling, no concern, and no worry.

The change was sudden, like flipping a switch.

"Ms. Matheson," Mercer said. "Nice to see you."

"Mercer." Fiona looked from him to Megan, smiling, then back to him. "How's the car coming along?"

"One day at a time." He half turned to Megan. "Mrs. Stokes here was good enough to provide an excuse to take a break and let me walk with her."

"I didn't realize you two knew each other."

"We met the day you had to work," Megan said. "I saw him outside today, so I decided to stop and say hello."

"You know"—Fiona pointed to Mercer—"maybe you can take a look at her car."

"No," Megan said. "I don't want to impose—"

"He's a fantastic mechanic," Fiona said. "And it wouldn't hurt to get a second opinion."

Mercer looked at Megan. "Are you having car troubles?"

She told him about breaking down in Ashland and what the mechanic at the garage told her.

"I'll be happy to take a look," he said. "But if the engine is seized, it's probably not worth fixing."

Fiona winked at her.

"We still need to have it towed," Megan said. "And I don't want it to be a hassle."

"Not a hassle at all."

There was a moment of strained silence. Then Mercer motioned to Fiona's clipboard. "Ashland?"

Fiona held out the clipboard. "You didn't change your mind about helping this year, did you?"

Mercer shook his head. "I'm afraid not, but try me next time."

Fiona looked at Megan and rolled her eyes. "He always says the same thing, every time I ask."

"One of these days, I promise." He smiled and glanced at his watch. "Well, I suppose I should head home."

"I didn't mean to interrupt," Fiona said. "I'm just tracking down volunteers. Don't let me barge in."

"Not at all," Mercer said. "I have a few things I wanted to work on before the sun went down."

"Remember," Fiona said. "You promised me a ride."

"And you'll get it." He turned to Megan. "Thank you for the company and the conversation, Mrs. Stokes."

"Oh, your books." Fiona snapped her fingers, looked at Megan. "Did he tell you he was a writer?"

"He mentioned it."

"Megan is having a tough time finding books to read around here."

"Borrow some of mine," Mercer said. "I have boxes of them in my basement. Stop by and take your pick. I'll lend you as many as you'd like."

Megan thanked him, told him she would.

"Why don't you let her read one of your books?" Fiona looked at Megan and shuddered. "Creepy stuff."

"Would you mind?"

"If you'd like," he said. "Although you might not be my audience."

"You don't know that," Megan said. "What kind of books do you write?"

Mercer looked from Megan to Fiona and then back. "The kind where nothing is as it seems."

24

M egan stood with Fiona at the edge of the willow forest and watched Mercer walk away. All the things he told her were still spinning in her head, and she went over them again and again, searching for anything that didn't fit with what she'd seen.

Bringing people back from the dead?

Was it possible?

Once Mercer was out of earshot, Fiona leaned in and whispered, "He hasn't been the same since his wife died."

Megan wasn't sure what to say, so she kept quiet.

"She worked at the Institute when I first came here," Fiona said. "She was one of their top engineers."

"What happened to her?"

Fiona's jaw muscle twitched, and she shook her head. "I'm not sure exactly. All I know is that her loss was a blow to everyone around here."

"It was nice of the Institute to let him stay," Megan said. "I'm not sure I would've wanted to if I were him."

Fiona nodded. "Speaking of neighbors, I went by the Addison place this morning and spoke to Roger."

Megan looked up, all thoughts of Mercer gone.

"What did he say?"

"Same thing he said to you." She put her hand on the clipboard. "I told him I was looking for Rachel, and he said she's visiting her sister in San Francisco. I have to say, he sounded sincere."

"Did you notice anything strange at all?"

"No, but I didn't want to seem obvious about it, either. He invited me in for a cup of coffee, and while he was making it, I did a little snooping."

"And?"

Fiona shook her head. "Nothing out of the ordinary. I'm sorry."

She nodded, looked away.

"I asked if Rachel was okay, and I mentioned that she seemed to be acting a little strange lately."

"And?"

"He dodged the question. He made the excuse that he'd been out of town a lot recently, and that she'd been upset about it, but otherwise she was fine."

Megan laughed under her breath. "That's a lie."

"He made it sound like her visit to her sister's was the direct result of him being gone so much," she said. "Everyone knows they don't have the closest marriage, so her leaving out of the blue isn't all that suspicious."

"Except she didn't leave," Megan said. "At least not on her own. They took her out of that house. I saw it."

Fiona was silent.

"You still don't believe me?"

"I didn't say that," Fiona said. "And this is only a first step. We'll keep our eyes open and ask questions. If something is going on, we'll figure it out."

Megan started to point out that she hadn't answered her question, but she didn't want to put her on the spot.

Instead, she told her she was right.

"So, what did you and Mercer talk about?" Fiona asked, changing the subject. "He doesn't usually open up to people like that. He must like you. What's your secret?"

"I complimented his car."

Fiona laughed. "Of course."

The sound made Megan smile.

For a brief moment, she thought about telling Fiona about her conversation with Mercer, about the experiments he believed they were running at the Institute, and about the documents he claimed to have hidden away in the forest that would prove all of it.

But she didn't.

Fiona was the only friend she had, and right now she was on her side, but her trust felt fragile. Megan wanted to decide on her own what she thought of Mercer's story before mentioning anything to Fiona.

Also, she'd made a promise.

Fiona walked with her back toward her house. Along the way, Megan noticed several people standing at their windows watching them, but when she pointed one of them out, Fiona just smiled and waved to them, then changed the subject.

"How did it go with Tyler after I dropped you off?"

"Better than I expected," Megan said. "He knew I was trying to leave."

"You're kidding?"

"He didn't say anything about it directly, but I could tell. He's not stupid."

"What did he say?"

"I told him about the car, and we talked about getting a second opinion. That's about it."

"And you didn't say anything to him about Rachel?"

"Only that I didn't want to talk about her anymore."

"Good," Fiona said. "I'm going to dig a little deeper, maybe visit a few of the neighbors and see if anyone noticed anything before she left."

"Before they took her."

"My point is, I'll see what I can find out while you lay low and let that wound heal a bit with your husband."

"I'll try."

Fiona put her hand on Megan's arm. "Don't worry. We'll figure this out, and I'm sure it'll all make sense in the end."

———

That night, Tyler came home early. Megan grilled salmon and asparagus for dinner, and they took everything out back and ate together on the deck. By the time they finished, the sun was going down and a silent scatter of fireflies floated just above the lawn.

Megan watched them and thought about Mercer and Rachel and the Institute on top of the ridge.

"Where are you?"

Tyler's voice pulled her back. "What?"

"You're far away tonight," he said. "I was wondering where you were. What are you thinking?"

Megan reached for her wineglass and leaned back in her chair. "What exactly do you do?"

"What do you mean?"

"Your job," she said. "What do you do?"

"You know what I do."

"I know you're a technician and that you fix things when they break, but that's about it."

"There's not much else to know," he said. "Most of the time I run diagnostic programs, and if anything pops up, I either fix the issue or assign it to a different group."

"Diagnostic programs on what?"

"All the proprietary hardware and software up there." Tyler frowned. "You've never cared about my job before. Why the sudden interest?"

"I was thinking about you today," she said. "Every time I look up at the ridge I wonder what you're doing, so I decided to ask."

Tyler's eyes narrowed.

"What?" she asked. "Something wrong with wanting to know what my husband does with his days?"

"No, it's just unusual for you."

Megan knew she'd made him suspicious.

She also knew that all she had to do was take his hand, tilt her head, and raise the pitch of her voice while making some excuse about wanting to get closer to him, and his suspicion would fade away. But she'd never been good at that kind of thing.

Besides, she wanted to know more about the Institute.

"Do you ever see Fiona?" Megan asked.

"Your friend?"

"She works up there, too. Some kind of administrative supervisor or something."

"I don't have contact with anyone on that level unless something breaks. And when that happens, they usually send someone else. I'm still the new guy up there."

"Have you ever seen anything weird?"

"What do you mean?"

"The Hansen Institute—they do all kinds of medical research, don't they? That's pretty interesting. Have you ever seen anything strange?"

Tyler inhaled deeply and leaned forward, resting his forearms on the table. "Megs, I spend my days in a room without windows, staring at numbers on a screen. I compare those numbers to other numbers on a different screen. When they match, my job is easy. When they don't match, I make a phone call to someone I never see. So no, I've never seen anything I think you'd consider interesting."

"That's really all you do?"

Tyler looked at her, his eyes hard. "I'm an entry-level systems technician. What did you think I did?"

"I don't know," she said. "I just thought with everything they do up there that you'd have seen—"

"What is this about?" he asked. "Why the sudden interest in my job?"

There was a sharpness to his voice, and Megan realized she'd pushed too far. Without thinking, she put her hand on his, tilted her head, and said, "I want to know more about what you do," the pitch of her voice lifting each word. "I want to be closer to you, to try and make things better."

Tyler stared at her for a moment, and she saw the softness slowly come back to his face. She leaned in, kissed him, and smiled.

"I'm sorry," he said. "It's been a tough week. I'm a little on edge."

She told him it was fine, that she didn't take it personally. Then she reached for the wine bottle and refilled his glass, smiling, and thinking that she'd underestimated herself.

25

The next morning, Megan woke to Tyler standing over the bed, watching her sleep.

She sat up slowly, her voice tired. "Hey."

Tyler was dressed for work, his coffee mug in one hand, and his keys dangling loose in the other.

He didn't say anything.

"What are you doing?" Megan asked.

"Leaving for work," he said. "I'll probably be late tonight. Thought you should know."

"Okay." Megan's head was still clouded, and her thoughts were thick and slow. "Is everything okay?"

"Yeah." He forced a smile. "It's a busy week."

"I mean with you. Is everything okay with—"

"I'm fine," he said. "I wanted to see you before I left. You might be asleep when I get home."

Megan eased back down onto the bed and rubbed her

eyes. She didn't believe his excuse, and she tried not to let it show.

"You're sweet," she said.

"Are you seeing your friend today?"

"My friend?"

"Fiona?"

"I was thinking about stopping by her house this afternoon. Why?"

"No reason." He stared at her for a moment longer, then leaned down and kissed the top of her head. "Maybe I'll see you later tonight."

Before Megan could reply, he turned and walked out.

She stayed in bed, listening to his footsteps on the stairs. She waited until she heard the front door close, then she got up and walked to the window and watched him back down the driveway and into the road.

There was a hollow space growing in her chest. She tried to ignore it, but the more she thought about the way Tyler sounded, the way he looked at her, the wider it got.

Something was wrong.

Why did he ask about Fiona?

Megan took her robe off the back of the door and slipped it on. Then she walked downstairs to the kitchen, picked up the phone, and dialed Fiona's number. She let it ring for a long time before hanging up.

The empty feeling in her chest spread, and it was too strong to shake. She told herself she was being paranoid, that she and Tyler had been through a lot lately, and it was going to take some time before things seemed normal again.

She was looking for problems where none existed.

The idea calmed her a little.

Megan put the phone back in the cradle, then took her coffee cup from the dish drainer and reached for the coffeepot.

It was empty.

Megan frowned and started another pot.

While she waited for the coffee to brew, she went into the living room and stood at the window and looked out at the street, thinking about what she needed to do.

Fiona was going to ask around about Rachel, and while she would've loved to join her, Fiona had already said she'd handle it on her own.

That left Mercer.

After their conversation the day before, Megan had even more questions. She wanted him to show her the documents he had hidden in the forest. If they proved what he said they proved, Tyler would have to believe her.

Megan glanced over at Rachel's house. The curtains were all open to the sunlight, and the roses out front were in full bloom. Roger's car was gone, and she wondered, not for the first time, what he was hiding.

Megan was so lost in her thoughts that she didn't notice Rachel sitting outside on the grass next to the rosebushes. It wasn't until she stood up and crossed the yard toward the garage that Megan realized she was there at all.

Her breath caught in her throat.

Rachel was wearing her white sun hat and her tortoiseshell sunglasses, and she seemed to shimmer like a mirage between the green lawn and the blue sky.

In the kitchen, the coffeemaker beeped.

Megan barely heard it.

Rachel disappeared into the garage, and Megan stayed at the window. When Rachel came back, she was carrying a flat wicker basket, her arm looped through the handle. Megan watched as she moved down the length of the rosebushes, carefully selecting and cutting the best flowers before laying them lengthwise in the basket.

Megan backed away from the window and headed for the front door. She stopped at the bottom of the porch steps and checked to see that Rachel was still outside. Then she started across the street toward her house.

Megan's feet were bare, and the ground was sharp, but she stayed focused on Rachel and ignored the pain. The closer she got, the less real it all seemed.

As if she would wake up at any moment.

When Megan got to her house, she stepped onto Rachel's lawn and came up behind her. She lifted her hand and gently touched the back of Rachel's neck, still not believing she was real.

Rachel jumped, startled, and turned around.

"Oh my." She put a hand to her chest, her eyes wide and panicked. "Megan, you scared me half to death."

Megan felt her mouth open, but no words came out.

"You have to let me catch my breath." Rachel's voice was sunshine, and she exhaled loud and musically. "It's so nice to see you."

"You're back."

"Since late last night," she said. "I'd ask if I missed anything exciting, but who am I kidding?"

Rachel laughed, then looked down at the flowers in her basket. She selected one and held it out to Megan. "What do you think?"

Megan took the flower. It was bright yellow.

"Careful of the thorns."

Megan stared at her, unable to speak.

Rachel stepped closer and slipped off her sunglasses. Her skin was soft, and her eyes were clear and blue.

"Are you feeling okay, honey?"

She didn't answer.

Rachel glanced down at Megan's bare feet, then around at the other houses lining the street. She set the basket on the ground and took Megan's arm, leading her back toward her house.

"Can I share some advice, dear?" Her voice was a sweet whisper. "My mother had a rule. She used to tell me that the distance between your front door and your mailbox is the exact same distance you can go outside in your robe before people start thinking you're a crazy person."

"You're not dead."

Rachel stopped walking. "Excuse me?"

"You fell off the ladder," Megan said. "I saw—"

"I did what?"

"You lost your balance. You broke your neck."

Rachel laughed, her eyes sharp, but confused.

Megan was about to say something else, but then the expression on Rachel's face softened and she smiled.

"I believe you had a dream, my dear." She held Megan at arm's length. "It looks as though you might have just woken up, and I believe—"

Megan pulled away, backing across the lawn toward the sidewalk. Rachel watched her, frowning. Then she turned and went back to her rosebushes.

Megan ran the rest of the way home, her robe billowing out behind her. She had to talk to Fiona. She had to tell her about Rachel, but when she got home and called her house, there was still no answer.

Megan hung up the phone and leaned against the counter, breathing hard. She didn't know where to turn, and her mind was racing. She could feel her thoughts spinning away, and she knew she had to get out of the house.

Megan went upstairs to shower.

She stood under the water for a long time, letting the heat sink into her skin, thinking about her options.

There weren't many, and she didn't like any of them.

PART III

26

M ercer's garage was open, and the car inside was covered with a dull gray tarp. Megan was hoping to see him outside, but the house was silent. All around her, the leaves of the trees shook in the wind, and a line of heavy clouds moved in overhead, as if building for rain.

She walked up the path toward Mercer's front door and rang the bell. Then she stepped back, waiting.

The woman who answered the door looked to be in her late forties. She had blond hair and brown roots, and wore thick-rimmed glasses. She smiled when she saw Megan, but there was nothing friendly about it.

"Yes?"

"I'm looking for David Mercer."

"What's this regarding?"

Megan wasn't sure what to say, and she stumbled over her words. "I'm a friend of his. He asked me to stop by."

"You're a friend of Mercer's?"

"That's right. Is he home?"

The woman stood in the doorway, watching her. Then she shook her head and said, "Well, you just missed him. He left this morning for a car show in Denver."

"He's gone?"

"Afraid so."

"I just spoke to him yesterday," Megan said. "He never mentioned a car show, or that he was leaving."

"That doesn't surprise me," the woman said. "There's Dad and his plans, and then there's everyone else."

"You're his daughter?"

The woman nodded. "If you'd like, I can leave him a note and let him know you stopped by. I'm only here for a day or two."

"How long will he be gone?"

"I honestly don't know," she said. "With him it could be a day, or a month if he gets distracted." Megan paused, then looked up at the swirling clouds.

The woman followed her gaze, frowning. "Better make up your mind," she said. "Looks like you're going to get wet."

"Will you let him know that I came by?" she asked. "My name is Megan. He was expecting me."

The woman's eyebrows rose. "Megan Stokes?"

"That's right."

"I think he left something for you. Hang on a minute."

She let the screen door close, leaving her alone on the

porch. Megan walked toward the steps and stared out at the street. A gray Mercedes drove by, and for an instant she thought she saw a young girl in the backseat, staring out at her as they passed, but it was only a reflection, light on the glass.

"Here you go."

The woman was back, standing in the doorway. She had a book in her hand, holding it out. Megan took it and turned it over. There was a large black rabbit on the cover, silhouetted by a golden-orange sunset.

Watership Down.

"He left this for me?"

The woman held up a yellow sticky note with Megan's name scribbled on it in pencil.

"This you?"

Megan told her it was.

"Then he left it for you." The woman crumpled the note and squeezed it in her thick fist. "I'll let him know you were here next time I speak to him."

"Thank you."

Megan walked down the path and stopped on the sidewalk. She didn't want to think about Mercer being gone the day after they'd talked, or what that might mean. If she allowed herself to go down that road, she wasn't sure she'd be able to get back.

Instead, she looked down and read the text on the back of the book. Then she flipped it over and fanned through the pages.

The book opened to the middle, and a small brass key pressed inside.

Megan closed the book fast and glanced back at Mercer's house. The woman was standing at the window, watching her, but when she saw her looking, she stepped away and faded back into the dark room.

Megan put her head down and started walking.

———

She climbed the steps to Fiona's front door and rang the bell. While she waited, she moved to the edge of the porch and stared up at the tumbling sky and the gray swirl of clouds.

You're going to get wet.

Megan glanced down at the book and opened it, letting the key slide out into her palm. It was a plain key, brass and ordinary, and she turned it over a few times, examining both sides for any numbers or markings.

All she saw were scratches and age.

Her hands started to shake, and she dropped the key into her front pocket, then rang the bell again. She didn't hear any sounds inside, so she stood on her toes and looked in through the small windows at the top of the door.

The house was dark.

They got to Fiona, too.

The thought dug in before she could stop it, and a slow chill wormed its way along the base of her spine. She told herself that Fiona was at work, or maybe running errands, and there wasn't anything to worry about.

All she had to do was wait for her to get back.

Megan wanted to believe it.

She sat at the top of the porch steps and looked around at the pastel houses along the street, all of them several shades dimmer under the heavy clouds. In the distance, she could see the edge of the forest, and it made her think of the spot Mercer pointed out the day before, and about the path leading through the trees toward the abandoned shed with the lockbox hidden inside.

She felt for the key in her pocket.

Mercer had given it to her for a reason. He'd wanted her to go to the shed and find what he'd hidden, even told her where to look.

Did he know he wouldn't be going with her?

She took the key from her pocket and held it between her fingers. She wanted to know what was inside the shed, but she didn't want to go alone. Whatever she found, this time she needed a witness.

She needed Fiona.

Megan glanced down the empty street, and once again the fear that Fiona was gone seeped into her mind. She thought of her talking to the neighbors, asking around about Rachel, drawing attention.

Disappearing.

Like Mercer, suddenly gone the day after telling her about his wife and what she did at the Institute.

Both of them had been removed.

Megan shook the thought away the best she could. Then she slipped the key back into her pocket. She knew she was letting her imagination get the best of her, and she tried to laugh it off, telling herself that she'd read too many bad books.

But after everything that'd happened, everything she'd seen, she didn't feel much like laughing.

Megan pushed herself up and started down the steps. When she got to the bottom, she noticed a woman standing across the street. She was alone in her empty driveway, two houses down, wearing black pants and a black button-up shirt. Her hands were at her sides, and her hair, plain and brown, moved back and forth with the wind.

She was staring at her.

Megan waved, but the woman didn't wave back.

Then, out of the corner of her eye, Megan saw movement in the house next door and glanced over. There was a man watching her from the window, his face barely visible behind the glass.

And there were others.

At all the houses along the street, in nearly every window, someone was looking back at her.

She decided it was time to go.

M egan walked home, head down, and even though she didn't see anyone else, she could feel eyes on her the entire way. She tried to tell herself that it was all in her head and that no one was really watching, but the sensation was too strong, and she couldn't shake it.

Once she was inside, she went upstairs to the bathroom and sat on the edge of the tub, squeezing her hands between her knees to stop them from shaking.

After a while, she got up and paced back and forth in the hallway. Her stomach ached, and all she wanted was to run away, far and fast, until she couldn't run anymore. She wanted to be exhausted, numb, and she didn't want to have to think about any of this anymore.

She wanted to forget.

The phone rang, and Megan stopped pacing. On the second ring, she hurried downstairs to the kitchen and stood over the phone. She started to reach for the receiver, but something stopped her. Then, on the fifth ring, she forced herself to pick it up.

"Hello?"

There was no response.

She tried again. "Hello?"

This time, she heard someone shuffle on the other end, but still, no one spoke. Megan pulled the phone away from her ear and hung up. Her chest tightened. She tried to calm down and take deep breaths, but the air only came in short, hitching gasps.

The room wavered around her. She had enough time to think, *I'm hyperventilating,* before the strength ran out of her legs and she slipped down to the floor.

She didn't pass out, but she also didn't move for a long time. All she could do was sit there and try to steady her breath, while tears ran down her cheeks, dropping dark into her lap.

All the bad thoughts came back to her, one after the other, and she couldn't stop them. There was nowhere for her to turn, no one to talk to.

Fiona was missing, Mercer was gone, and Tyler . . .

Tyler didn't trust her.

She knew he would still come running if she called, but not the way she wanted him to. He would try to calm her down, but then he'd push her toward therapy or medication. He wouldn't listen to her, not this time, not after everything that'd happened.

Not unless she had proof.

The thought stuck.

Megan looked up at the clock on the stove and counted the hours left until dark. Then she grabbed the edge of the counter and pulled herself up off the floor. She stood for a moment, making sure her legs were steady. Then she walked into the living room and lay back on the couch, listening to the grandfather clock ticking steadily in the corner.

Megan closed her eyes and waited.

———

Once the sun went down, Megan left the house.

She walked along the street toward the forest at the base of the ridge. She had a flashlight with her, but the batteries were old, and the bulb was dim.

Still, it was better than nothing.

The neighborhood felt deserted, and her footsteps echoed in the still night air. She kept an eye out for anyone watching her as she walked, but all she saw were dark windows and empty streets.

When Megan reached the forest, she searched for the spot Mercer had pointed out the day before. Once she found the electrical box, she took one last look at the houses along the street. Then she crossed the short stretch of grass toward the woods.

Mercer had said there would be a path, and that it would lead into the forest and down to the creek where she would find the shed.

But there was no path.

The deeper into the woods she went, the more she wondered if this was nothing more than an old man's idea of a joke.

She was about to turn back when she noticed a slight indentation in the weeds between the trees. Megan shone her light on the spot and followed it. After several yards, the undergrowth split and the path became clear.

Megan knew she should be happy, but there was a hollow pain in the pit of her stomach, and it made her wonder if a part of her had hoped it had been a lie.

Sometimes, she thought, crazy was easier.

In the distance, she heard the low rumble of thunder, and she tried not to think about rain. The wind picked up, and the trees bent and swayed around her as she followed the path deeper into the woods.

Then she heard the river.

After a few more yards, she saw it.

Megan stopped on the edge and looked out over the slow black water. She could see the shadows of the willow trees on the other side of the bank, their low branches touching the surface, dragging along with the current.

Her flashlight flickered, and she smacked it with her hand to make it stop. Then she panned the forest, searching for Mercer's shed, but all she saw were trees and shadows.

"You've got to be kidding."

The hollow pain in her stomach faded, replaced by frustration and anger.

There was no shed, no lockbox. She'd wasted her time, and she was no closer to understanding anything.

Maybe, she thought, she really had lost her mind.

Megan felt the first drop of rain touch her face, and she wiped it away. Then she looked down at the path leading toward the street. She considered giving up and going back, but she wasn't quite ready to let go yet.

If Mercer lied, why did he give her a key?

She didn't have an answer, and that was enough for her to keep looking.

Megan stepped off the path and followed the riverbank farther into the forest, hoping her flashlight would last. If it died while she was off the path, finding her way back in the dark would be a challenge.

Lightning flashed, turning the trees blue.

Then she saw it.

The shed was off to her right, partially hidden under a wall of creeper vines. Megan moved closer, circling it, shining her light over the surface.

It was smaller than she'd expected, no bigger than a walk-in closet. The wood was weatherworn and warped, and several shingles were missing from the roof. The creeper vines were thick, covering one side and hanging down over the front.

Megan pushed the vines aside and reached for the rusted metal door handle and pulled.

The door creaked open easily.

The shed was empty.

She stood there for a long time, the dim light from her flashlight trailing over the empty walls and the wooden planked floor. Slowly, the reality of the situation sank in, and she laughed.

The sound was loud, but she didn't care. There was no one around to hear, and once she got started, she couldn't stop. She didn't want to stop.

A minute later, the rain started to fall.

Heavy drops splintered through the canopy of leaves above her, boiling over the surface of the river.

Megan thought about making a run for the path, but the storm had quickly turned into a downpour. If she went back, she'd be soaked through by the time she made it home.

Instead, she stepped into the shed.

Even with the missing shingles, the inside of the shed stayed dry. Megan shut off her flashlight, eased herself down to the floor, and stared out at the rain and the trees and waited. After a while, she felt tears on her cheeks, but she told herself it was just the rain.

The storm didn't last.

Eventually, the rain thinned, and the heavy rattle of water hitting the roof slowed. If she started back, she figured she'd still get wet, but at least she wouldn't get drenched, and that was fine.

Megan leaned forward and pushed herself up.

As she stood, one of the boards under her hand slid an inch to the side.

She looked down.

There was an empty space between the boards, and through it, Megan could see a dull shine of metal in the near dark.

Once again, a wave of laughter rose in her chest, but this time she kept it inside.

All she did was smile.

28

M egan pulled the loose boards away and reached inside, grabbing the handle on the top of the lockbox. It came out easily, and she set it on the floor next to her.

The box was gunmetal gray and covered with what looked like years of dirt. Megan brushed it off with the side of her hand, then shone her flashlight on the lock and tried the key.

It slid in easily, and she opened the lid.

There were a few manila files inside, yellowed by age, and a folded developer's map. When she took them out, two Polaroid photographs slipped free and fell into her lap.

She held them up to the flashlight.

The images had degraded a bit, but they were still clear enough to see.

One of the photographs had been taken outside the Hansen Institute. In it, two men and a woman, all wearing white lab coats, stood in a half circle. Behind them, a large group of men and women, also in white lab coats, were lined up in front of the entrance to the Institute, their arms at their sides, their faces blurred by time.

Megan flipped to the other Polaroid and shone her flashlight on the image.

She recognized what it was immediately.

The shot had been taken from the top of the ridge, looking east toward the horizon. On the white bar at the bottom of the photo, in blue ink, someone had written:

Willow Ridge Development Project.

Megan squinted, looked closer.

In the photo, several of the houses had already been built. There were cement trucks and earth-moving equipment scattered in among the unpaved roads and new foundations. At the far edge of the photo, she could just make out a thin line of highway, CR-11, cutting through farmland toward Ashland.

She set the photos on the ground next to her and picked up the map. She unfolded it under the light.

It looked like a site plan for Willow Ridge. All the streets were in place, and the houses were marked as individual units. The entire neighborhood had been divided into several sections over a large grid.

Megan studied it for a minute, then refolded the map and set it on the ground next to the photos. Then she turned to the manila files. There were five of them. Each one had a name written along the top. One of the names was too smeared to read, but the others were clear.

Claire Nelson.
Nicholas Bartlett.
David Mercer.
Edna Davidson.

Megan stopped on Edna Davidson's file and stared at the name. For the first time, she felt like she was prying into something that she had no business seeing, and a part of her didn't want to open it.

But it was a small part.

She separated Edna's file from the others and set them next to the photos. Then she opened the folder. There were two sheets of wrinkled and faded carbon paper inside, and she had to hold the light close to make out what was written on the pages.

The first sheet looked like a hospital admission form with the Hansen Institute logo in the upper-right corner and the company address in the upper left. The page was divided into several sections:

PATIENT'S NAME, ADDRESS, DATE OF BIRTH, and MEDICAL HISTORY.

Megan read through them all, then stopped.

The last box, along the bottom of the page, was labeled: CAUSE OF DEATH. And below it, typed in faded blue letters, were the words: *Metastatic breast cancer.*

Megan's mouth was dry, and she swallowed hard.

She flipped to the second page.

At the top of the page was one word:

TREATMENT.

There were several handwritten notes, but most were too faint to read under the dim flashlight. Megan struggled for a while, then gave up and closed the file. She reached down and fanned through the other folders until she found the one for David Mercer.

She pulled it free and opened it on her lap.

Again, there were two pages inside.

Megan scanned to the bottom of the first sheet to the section labeled: **CAUSE OF DEATH**. When she read what was written, she felt like she'd been kicked in the chest.

One word:

Suicide.

He'd told her the truth.

The realization sighed out of her, and she hesitated for a moment before turning the page.

The second page was faded, but not as bad as Edna's. She could read the word **TREATMENT** at the top, and below it several sections of handwritten notes, all dark enough to see in the fading light.

Phase One: Experimental
Intrathecal bioactive peptides.

Mesenchymal stem cell therapy.

Phase Two: Reactive

Transcranial IV laser phototherapy.

Median nerve stimulation.

Phase Three: Outcome

Reversal: Complete

Observation section: X3, Unit 11b, Grid 16a.

Designated safety concern: Negative

The rest of the notes were no more than snaking lines and dates, and they were impossible for her to read.

Megan opened the last two files and scanned the pages. They were mostly faded like the others, but what she was able to read matched what she'd already seen.

When she finished, she stacked the files on her lap, then reached for the photographs and the map and slipped them inside Mercer's file. She checked the lockbox one more time for anything she might've missed, but it was empty.

Megan listened to the last of the rain falling on the roof of the shed. Then she looked out the open door at the trees swaying in the shadows, trying to make sense out of what she'd found.

Mercer had told her the truth.

This thought opened the door for another.

If Mercer's file was true, then the others had to be true. The Institute had found a way to reverse death, and they were experimenting on the people in Willow Ridge.

She thought about Rachel and everything that'd happened

since that night in the garage.

All the pieces seemed to fit.

Outside, the rain stopped.

Megan got up, slipped the files under her arm, and walked out of the shed. Above her, the sky was still clouded, but she could see a few breaks through the trees where the stars had begun to burn through.

She stood there, staring up at the sky, and listened to the soft rumble of the creek. For the first time in a long time, her mind was quiet, and her body felt light.

When she was ready, Megan took a deep breath and followed the flashlight back to the path. Halfway through the forest, the dying light flickered and went out.

Megan walked the rest of the way in darkness.

She didn't like it, and when she got close enough to Willow Ridge to see the amber streetlights shining through the trees, she was almost relieved.

29

Tyler's car wasn't in the driveway when Megan got home, and even though she hated to admit it, she was happy he wasn't there. She needed time to regroup before showing him what she'd found.

The thought that he wouldn't believe her worried her, but she didn't think that would happen, not anymore, not after he saw the files. She might not be able to fill in all the blanks yet, but what she'd found was a start.

It had to be enough.

Megan crossed the yard and went in through the front door. She didn't take off her coat or her shoes. Instead, she went into the kitchen and set the files on the table, spreading them out, searching for anything that might make Tyler think they were fakes.

Nothing stood out, so she put them all together and stacked them in front of her. Then she picked up the photos.

She glanced at the one labeled: *Willow Ridge Development Project*, then the group photo of the blurred people standing outside the Institute.

She stared at their faces for a long time.

———

When Tyler came home, Megan was still in the kitchen, standing at the window and looking out toward the backyard. The bottle of bourbon was on the counter, and she had a drink in her hand, but she'd barely touched it.

She wanted her head to be clear.

When she heard Tyler's keys in the lock, she poured her drink into the sink and turned on the faucet to rinse it away. She felt a cold stab of nervousness in the pit of her stomach, but it passed quickly.

"Megan?"

"In the kitchen."

She leaned back against the counter and listened to his footsteps coming down the hall, her heart beating hard. He came through the doorway, slowly, and when he saw her, he crossed the room, then leaned in and kissed her cheek.

"How was your day?"

The files and the photographs were sitting on the table, but he didn't notice them right away. Megan tilted her head up at him.

"We have to talk."

The muscles in Tyler's shoulders sagged, and he leaned

against the counter next to her. When he spoke, his voice was tired.

"I don't know what to say anymore."

"You don't have to say anything," Megan said. "I want you to look at something and help me understand."

Tyler's eyes narrowed.

Megan pointed to the table and the files stacked on the surface. "There."

"What are those?"

"I was hoping you'd know."

Tyler hesitated, then pushed away from the counter and crossed the kitchen. He stood over the table and reached down, fanning the files out. Then he picked up one of the photographs, saw what it was, and looked at Megan.

"Am I going to need a drink for this?"

Megan went to the cabinet and grabbed a glass from the shelf. Then she opened the freezer and took out two ice cubes. She dropped them in the glass and reached for the bottle on the counter and poured.

Tyler pulled the chair away from the table and sat down. He took the first file and opened it as Megan set the drink next to him.

"I can't read these," he said. "What are they?"

"Look at the top. That's the Institute logo." She reached over and pushed through the files. "Here, this one. Read the name."

Tyler studied the pages in the file, shook his head.

"It's Edna," Megan said. "Next door."

"Are these her medical records?"

"That's what I thought, but look." She took the top page and pointed to the bottom section. "Cause of death."

"I don't understand."

"And then here." She flipped to the next page and tapped it with her finger. "You have to hold them up to the light to see, but these are all treatments. Some kind of experiments they ran on her. They have everything listed, even the location of her house."

"Her address?"

"Not her address, the location." Megan grabbed the site plan and unfolded it over the files. "Willow Ridge is divided into sections. The entire neighborhood is set up in a grid, and all the houses are marked as individual units."

"I still don't—"

"They're tracking her." Megan put her hand on the stack of files. "All these people, and probably more. They're experimenting on them and studying them, right here, like lab rats."

Tyler frowned. "Where did you get these?"

"One of the neighbors had them hidden," she said. "Have you seen anything like this up there? Do you know—"

"One of the neighbors? Who?"

"It doesn't matter," she said. "But I'm not the only one who's seen things. Everything that happened with Rachel . . . it all makes sense if she's part of whatever experiments they're doing here."

Tyler looked down at the pages, then reached for another file. He studied it, shook his head. "These have to be fake. They're a joke. They can't be real."

"What are they doing at the Institute?" Megan asked. "You have to know something."

"Nothing like this," he said. "They have a department that designs medical equipment, but they're all engineers. They have a high-clearance R & D department in the main building, but they can't possibly . . ." Tyler's voice trailed off. He flipped through the other files, shaking his head. "These can't be real."

"They are real." Megan picked up Mercer's file. "This is who showed me where to find these files. His wife worked at the Institute from the beginning. She told him everything, and now they're watching him."

"Watching him? Why?"

"Because he remembers." She opened the file, pointed to the page. "Cause of death, suicide. He tried to kill himself, or he did kill himself. He has the scars on his wrists. But somehow they—"

"Saved his life?"

"Or brought him back." Megan frowned. "At least that's what he thinks, and that's what this file—"

"Megan, you can't believe all this."

"They did something to him." She pulled a chair away from the table and sat close to him. "Tyler, I saw Rachel die. Her neck was broken. A few days later she was outside, and she . . . she wasn't right."

Tyler didn't speak.

"That night when I fell asleep on the couch, I saw a team of people go into her house and take her away."

"You what?"

Megan waved the question away. "The next day Roger was home, and he told me she left town. Then a couple days later she's back, completely normal, and with no memory of any of it."

"Megan, this is crazy."

"After Mercer told me about these files, we were supposed to meet again, but when I went by his house, he was gone, out of town for some car show. Left without a word."

"So?"

"So if they were watching him—"

"You think the Institute took him?"

"Yes."

Tyler looked away.

"There's a pattern here, Tyler." She held up Mercer's folder. "Suicide." Picked up another. "Metastatic breast cancer." A third. "Myocardial infarction. All of these are listed as a cause of death, and I know for a fact that two out of these three people are still up and walking around out there, and I'm willing to bet the others are, too."

Tyler didn't say anything.

"Something is going on around here," Megan said. "Have you seen anything up there that—"

"I'm a systems technician, Megs. I work with numbers and databases. I haven't seen anything like this."

Megan sat back in her chair and stared off into the kitchen. For a while, they were both quiet. Then she looked over at him and asked, "What do biological technicians do?"

Tyler shrugged. He started to explain, but then the look in his eyes changed, and he shook his head.

"I guess I don't know exactly."

Megan sat up. "Is it possible—"

Tyler held up one hand. "Megan—"

"Something is happening here, and this is proof." She set her hand on the stack of files, then motioned toward the street. "Rachel is proof. Tyler, I know what I saw, and you have to believe me. Something is—"

Tyler put his hand on top of hers, squeezed.

Megan stopped talking.

"Okay," he said. "I believe you."

30

Megan wrapped her arms around Tyler's neck and held him for a long time. He rubbed her back, whispering, "It's okay. Everything's going to be okay."

When Megan let go, she tried to read his face, tried to see if he meant everything he was saying.

"What do you want to do?" he asked. "Tell me what will make you happy, and that's what we'll do."

She opened her mouth to tell him she wanted to leave, tonight, but she was scared to say the words, and they caught in her throat.

What if he says no?

Instead, she said, "You really believe me?"

Tyler looked down at the files on the table and picked one up. "I can't explain this. Any of it."

She reached out and touched his chin, moving his eyes gently back to her. "But you believe *me*?"

He stared at her for what seemed like a long time. "I can't say I don't have questions, but—I trust you."

"Then I want to leave." The words came in a rush, and once they were out, Megan felt clean. "I want to get in the car and go, tonight."

"Go where?" Tyler asked. "It's already so late."

"Home," she said. "But I don't care. As long as it's far away from here."

Tyler looked away and shook his head. When he turned back, she could see the sadness in his eyes.

"What's wrong?"

"This wasn't how I thought things would go," he said, his eyes wet. "I wanted to help, and I failed you. I'm sorry."

"Don't." She reached out, her hands on his cheeks, and kissed him. "It's going to be fine. We're going to be fine once we're back home. You didn't know what they were doing out here; how could you?"

He watched her, silent.

"They lied to us," she said. "But it's not too late to get out."

"What about the house? All of our things."

"We'll figure it out later," Megan said. "I'll go up and pack a bag to get us through the next week, and we'll worry about everything else once we're back in Chicago. I don't want to stay here."

Tyler looked around the room and nodded.

"Okay," he said. "You pack."

"What are you going to do?"

"I need to think for a minute." He held up his drink. "Finish this."

Megan wrapped her arms around him again. If it'd been possible, she would've let herself melt into him. When she let go, she ran upstairs without another word.

Megan opened the closet and took the suitcase off the top shelf and set it on the bed. It was the second time that week she'd packed, but this time, instead of fear, there was only joy and relief.

She divided the suitcase in half, filling both sides with underwear, T-shirts, and jeans. That would get them by for a while, and that was all that mattered.

Megan went into the bathroom and opened the medicine cabinet. She started gathering everything they'd need, and it didn't take long before her hands were full. On her way back to the bedroom, she heard a noise downstairs, and she stopped to listen.

Tyler was talking to someone.

Megan crossed the room to the bed and dropped everything on top of the suitcase. Then she walked out to the top of the stairs, holding her breath, trying to hear.

She was too far away to make out the words, so she crept down the steps, moving quietly. When she got to the bottom, she walked down the hallway toward the kitchen.

She could see Tyler's shadow on the floor, and she stopped

just outside the doorway, listening.

"That's right," Tyler said. "No, I don't think so . . ."

There was silence, and at first all she heard was the soft tick of the grandfather clock in the living room.

Then Tyler spoke again.

"She's upset, but not dangerous . . ." He paused. "Calmer . . . Yes, I think so . . . No, I understand . . . Okay, fifteen minutes."

Megan heard him hang up the phone, and for a moment she didn't know what to do. She listened as he turned on the faucet and rinsed his glass.

Then the anger came, hitting her hard.

———

She walked into the kitchen as Tyler was shutting off the water. He saw her over his shoulder and smiled. Then he reached for the dish towel above the sink and leaned back against the counter, drying his hands.

"Are we packed?" he asked.

Megan went to the phone and picked it up. She hit the redial button and held it to her ear, staring at him.

"What are you doing?" Tyler tossed the dish towel behind him and reached for the phone. "Megan, give me—"

"You lied to me!"

The phone rang and the line clicked.

At first there was nothing. Then a soft melody followed by three chimes and a light female voice.

"Hello, you have reached the admission office for the Hansen

Counseling Center. All operators are currently busy. Please hold for the next available representative."

A pause.

Then the voice repeated the message.

"Hello, you have reached the admission office for the Hansen Counseling Center. All operators are—"

She looked up at him, the rage building.

"What did you do?"

"Megs." Tyler reached out and took the phone from her, and she let him. He slid it back into the cradle. "There are people at the counseling center who we can talk to. They'll work with us, and they'll help us figure out what's wrong. All I want to do is help you—"

Megan swung, hard, her hand closed in a fist.

She struck Tyler just in front of his ear. He made a sound that was more shock than pain, and stepped back.

She charged him, still swinging.

A few more blows landed, but this time he was ready for them, and they didn't do much damage. Eventually, he managed to get hold of her wrists, and she stopped swinging.

"You lied to me!" she screamed at him, her throat ripping. "How could you lie to me?"

"Megan, stop it."

Tyler still had her wrists, but Megan jerked back and pulled free. She tried to run out of the kitchen, but he caught her from behind and wrapped his arms around her, lifting her off her feet and bringing her down hard against the kitchen counter.

Megan's head struck the cabinet, and she cried out.

For an instant, her vision faded, and the room swam behind her eyes. Tyler seemed to realize what he'd done, and his grip loosened.

It was just enough.

Megan pulled her arms free and tried to hit him again, swinging back with her elbows. Tyler stepped in, squeezing her around the chest, making it hard for her to breathe.

"Megan, stop," he said. "I'm trying to help you."

Again, she tried to spin out of his grip, but he was too strong, and he wouldn't let her turn. He put one hand on her back, between her shoulder blades, and pushed her down flat against the counter, pressing his weight against her, holding her in place.

"No one is going to hurt you," he said. "You have to calm down."

Megan tried to move, but he had her pinned tight.

She looked up and saw the phone in the cradle. It was close, and she grabbed for it. When she did, Tyler took his hand off her back and reached out, trying to stop her.

"Goddamn it, Megan, stop."

With his hand gone, Megan stood up and pushed herself off the counter. The back of her head struck Tyler's face, and she heard a soft crack. Out of the corner of her eye, she saw both his hands go up, covering his nose.

This was her chance.

She looked around for something she could use.

Anything.

She saw the knife block next to the stove, and she moved

quickly, grabbing one of the handles and pulling a steak knife from the line, blade down. She turned, swinging the knife hard, wanting to drive him back, to scare him long enough for her to get out of the house.

But Tyler was too close.

The blade struck him just below his right armpit and slipped between his ribs, sinking in up to the hilt.

All noise stopped.

Tyler's hands came away from his face, showing his bent and bloodied nose. He was making a ragged, wheezing sound, as if the air inside of him was being sucked out.

His eyes never left Megan.

He stepped away from her, his right arm half-raised, and looked down at the knife. Then, slowly, he reached over with his left hand, grabbed the handle, and pulled it out.

The blood came in a rush.

It poured out of him, a deep, nightmarish red, turning his white shirt dark and dripping wet on the floor.

He stared at the knife in his hand. Then he dropped it and looked up at Megan.

She stepped closer, tears running freely down her cheeks. "Oh, baby."

For a second, his eyes seemed to clear.

Tyler reached out to the counter for balance, missed, and slid down. He eased himself onto his back and lay there, his mouth opening and closing, as the blood swelled around him and pooled silently on the polished wood floor.

31

M egan watched the blood inch across the kitchen floor toward her feet. The room was strangely silent; even the ticking of the grandfather clock in the living room seemed to have stopped.

Then it all came rushing in.

Loud, like a scream.

She backed out of the kitchen and ran down the hall to the front door. When she got there, she stopped and paced the hallway, back and forth, her hands pressed against the sides of her head. She was talking to herself, but the words seemed to come all on their own, spitting out in an untethered rush of panic and jumbled thought.

Then, slowly, one thought rose above the others.

Fifteen minutes.

It was the last thing she'd heard Tyler say when he was on the phone.

Fifteen minutes.

Megan ran back to the kitchen and looked at the clock on the stove, but the numbers meant nothing to her. She didn't know how long it'd been, and the more she tried to figure it out, the more it slipped away from her.

She looked down at Tyler—motionless, his blood reflecting the light of the room—and tried to figure out what to do. Eventually, she walked carefully around him to the counter and picked up the phone.

Fiona would know what to do.

Fiona would help.

She put the phone to her ear and dialed Fiona's number.

The line clicked, and she waited.

But the phone didn't ring. Instead, a metallic buzz sounded, followed by a deep mechanical voice.

"Confirm. Grid nine. Unit seven. Access code: beta-one-seven-en-one. Confirm."

Megan dropped the phone on the counter. She stood there for a moment then turned and ran out of the kitchen and down the hall. Whoever Tyler had called, they were coming, and she had to hurry.

When Megan got to the door, she reached into the bowl for Tyler's keys, but the bowl was empty. Panic ripped through her, and she stepped back, looking around the room, trying to think of where his keys could be.

She didn't know where to start.

Megan closed her eyes and tried to clear her head. But

all she could think about was the slow, relentless pulse of the grandfather clock reminding her that she had to hurry.

Reminding her that they were coming.

His keys are in his pocket.

The second the thought came to her, Megan knew it was right. She ran back to the kitchen, but it wasn't until she stood over his body that the reality of how she had to get them sunk in.

Tyler was on his back, surrounded by blood.

Megan paused, then walked around to his left side and crouched over him, feeling her feet slip slightly in the blood.

She reached into his left pocket.

It was empty.

She moved closer, twisting to get her hand inside his right pocket. When her fingers touched the metal key ring, she sighed with relief.

She grabbed the ring with two fingers and tried to pull them out, but the keys caught on the fabric, and Tyler's body rocked back and forth with each try.

"Come on," she said. "Please."

Megan inched closer and reached deeper into his pocket for a better grip. This time, she got one finger through the ring, and she leaned back, pulling hard.

The keys moved.

Then her feet slipped out from under her and she fell backward, landing flat and hard.

The blood felt like warm oil under her hands.

Megan pushed herself up, fast, but it was too late. Her hands and legs were dripping red, and she could feel the blood soaking through her jeans to her skin.

She made a soft, wounded sound and stepped over Tyler toward the sink. As she reached for the faucet, something touched her leg, and she jumped back.

Tyler was looking up at her, his eyes clear and aware.

A scream caught in her throat, and Megan turned, almost slipping again, and ran out of the kitchen.

Out of the house.

Into the night.

———

Megan did her best to avoid streetlights, and whenever she heard a car or saw anyone, she would duck behind a tree or a hedge and keep out of sight until it was safe to move.

Slowly, she made her way to Fiona's house.

The blood on her clothes was already starting to dry, and Megan could hear the stiff, creaking sounds it made as she walked. She tried not to think about Tyler, but she couldn't quiet the voice inside her head, screaming at her, telling her he was still alive and that she needed to go back and help him.

But Tyler wasn't alive.

Tyler was part of the experiment.

Megan's ears were ringing, and she could feel the adrenaline running through her, making it impossible to think clearly. She focused on each step, concentrating only on reaching

Fiona's house. Nothing else mattered.

Fiona would know what to do.

Fiona would help.

As Megan came around the corner, she saw the edge of the forest along the foot of the ridge. Farther up, she could see Fiona's house in the middle of the block.

From where she stood, the house looked empty, and she felt a low pain in the center of her chest. If Fiona wasn't home, she didn't know what she was going to do.

She had no place else to go.

Megan kept her head down and started toward the house. As she got close, she noticed a young couple sitting on folding lawn chairs in the driveway next door. They both had tall glasses with long twisty straws in their hands, and both were leaning back, staring up at the stars.

Megan slipped behind a hedge and watched.

Neither of them moved.

She was starting to wonder if they were asleep, but then the man lifted his glass and sipped the drink through the straw before coughing and lowering the glass again.

Then he leaned back, eyes to the sky.

With them out front, and with her covered in blood, she knew she wouldn't be able to walk up to the front door and ring the bell.

She had to find a different way.

Megan glanced at the house beside her and ducked close to

the hedge. She ran through the yard to the next block and followed the sidewalk around to the street behind Fiona's house. Then she counted down from the corner and cut through into Fiona's backyard.

She stopped behind a cypress tree and watched the neighboring houses for any sign that she'd been seen. When she thought it was safe, she ran up to the back door, knocked on one of the small square windows, and waited.

When no one answered, she stepped back and looked up at the windows on the second floor.

They were all dark.

Silent.

Megan went back to the door and tried the knob. It was locked. She bent down and lifted the doormat, hoping for a hidden key, but saw only a clean spot on the cement.

Frustration swelled inside of her.

By now, whoever Tyler had called had shown up at her house. They'd found him in the kitchen, and they were without a doubt searching the neighborhood for her.

It was only a matter of time.

Megan looked down at the square windows on the door and pressed on the one closest to the knob. It didn't move, so she hit it with the palm of her hand.

Nothing.

She scanned the yard, searching for anything she could use. There was a hose coiled along the side of the house with a small metal sprinkler head attached to the end.

Megan unscrewed it and went back to the door.

For a second, she wondered if she really was losing her mind. The thought was so logical, and so late, that it almost made her laugh. And that made her want to cry.

But she didn't cry.

Instead, she stepped back and struck the small window with the end of the metal sprinkler.

The glass fell away, shattering easily.

32

M egan reached in through the broken window and unlocked the bolt. Then she pushed the door open and
stepped over the broken glass into Fiona's kitchen.

The house was quiet.

She stood at the edge of the kitchen and looked around.
The shadows coming through the windows above the sink
were sharp and black against the silver-blue light of the
moon.

"Fiona?"

She walked out into the hallway, moving slowly past the
living room toward the stairs and the door leading to the garage. Once again, she was struck by how strange it felt to be in
a house that was the mirror image of her own.

Megan stopped at the bottom of the stairs and looked up
toward the dark second floor. She thought about turning on a
light, but the last thing she wanted to do was draw attention.

"Fiona?"

She listened for a response and heard nothing. She started up the stairs, but then she remembered the blood on her hands and clothes and looked down. It was dry, but she didn't want to take the chance of leaving a trail.

Megan retraced her steps to the kitchen and crossed to the sink. She turned on the faucet and ran her hands under the water, scrubbing hard at the dark stains. There was a soap dispenser on the counter, but it was empty, so she checked the cabinet under the sink for more.

There was nothing under the sink.

Megan frowned, then stood up and shut off the water. She shook her hands dry, then opened the cabinet above the counter and looked inside.

Empty.

She moved down the line, opening drawers and cabinets, all of them empty. No dishes, no silverware, nothing.

Then Megan opened the cabinet next to the stove.

There was a wooden tray inside.

On top of the tray were two spoons, two blue-and-white china teacups, a sugar bowl, and a teapot. On the shelf above the tray were two boxes of tea, one yellow, one a pale green.

Megan thought back to the day Fiona found her outside Rachel's house and brought her here, the day she'd made tea, the day they'd talked until the sun went down.

Something inside her fell away.

"No."

Megan backed out of the kitchen and down the hallway. She went into the living room and opened every drawer on every piece of furniture, searching every closet.

All of them, empty.

She ran upstairs to the bathroom.

The medicine cabinet was empty, the towels clean and unused. She pulled the shower curtain back and grabbed the shampoo bottles off the ledge, each one hollow and light.

Megan made a sharp sound in the back of her throat and ran into the bedroom. She opened the closet, then checked the dresser drawers. All of them were empty.

Nothing is real.

The thought seemed to suck all the air out of her lungs, and she ran out of the bedroom toward the top of the stairs, her head spinning.

She wanted to get out of the house, but as she passed the doorway to Fiona's office, something on the wall caught her eye, and she stopped.

There was a map of Willow Ridge hanging beside her desk, framed in black and pressed flat behind glass.

Megan stepped into the room, moving closer, but even from a distance she knew what she was seeing. The map was the same site plan she'd found in the shed, the same one she'd shown Tyler before she . . .

Killed him . . .

She felt her throat tighten.

As she turned to leave, Megan noticed a stack of manila folders organized neatly on the top of the desk. She reached down and flipped through a few of the folders, then opened the top desk drawer. There were pens and clipboards inside along with several notepads. She took one out and thumbed through the pages. Every sheet was filled, top to bottom, with scribbled notes, times and addresses, and names.

Familiar names.

Megan dropped the notepad back in the drawer and glanced around the room. There were bookshelves along the far wall, stocked with books she didn't recognize, and a scatter of photographs of people Fiona had never mentioned. There was a diploma from Stanford University on the top shelf surrounded by several glass awards etched with the Institute logo and Fiona's name.

None of it made sense.

Once again, the urge to leave the house swept over her, but she pushed it away and ran out into the hallway and down the stairs. When she got to the kitchen, she crossed the room toward the phone mounted on the wall.

She picked up the receiver and held it to her ear.

Silence.

She hung up and tried again. Then she put the receiver back on the cradle, grabbed the phone with both hands, and slid it off the wall.

There was no cord attached.

Megan dropped the phone and stepped back, her hands

over her mouth. She didn't know if she wanted to scream or cry or just . . .

Run.

She was halfway to the front door when she heard a voice coming from the living room.

"Megan."

She jumped, spun around.

Fiona was in the living room, standing in front of the large bay window, and she wasn't alone. There were two men behind her on either side, both dressed in solid black.

Megan couldn't find her voice.

Then Fiona smiled, and that was all it took.

The words came flooding out, rolling over themselves in a desperate rush to be heard. Megan asked her about the house, the tea. Then she told her about Mercer and the files in the shed and about Rachel.

Fiona listened, patient and calm.

Then Megan told her about Tyler.

Tyler.

All at once, the reality of the situation swarmed around her, and she slid down to her knees.

The tears came hard, making it impossible to speak.

Fiona stepped closer, knelt beside her, and put a hand on her shoulder. "Megan," she said. "Everything is okay."

"No." She shook her head, her voice choked. "I killed him. I didn't mean to, but I did. The knife. He's dead."

"No, honey," she said. "Tyler is fine."

Megan looked up. "How can you say that?" She held out her hands, showing the blood on her clothes. "Look at this. Look at me."

Fiona reached down and took her hands, helping her to her feet. "You're going to have to trust me," she said. "You're going to have to believe that what I'm telling you is the truth."

When Megan got to her feet, she looked over Fiona's shoulder, past the two men standing in the living room and out the bay window toward the neighborhood.

There was a white van parked along the street.

"No."

Megan tried to pull away, but Fiona held her hands tight, gently shushing her.

"It's okay," she said. "You have to trust me."

"They're going to kill me," Megan said. "I know what's happening around here, and they're going to kill me."

Fiona frowned, but when she spoke, there was a kindness in her voice. "You don't know what's happening here, Megan. Not entirely. And I promise no one is going to kill you."

Megan barely heard her.

She tried again to pull her hands free, and she almost succeeded, but then Megan saw the two men behind Fiona step closer, and she stopped struggling.

Fiona held up a hand, and the men stepped back.

"Please," Megan said. "Help me."

"Of course I'll help you." Fiona took Megan's hands, pressing them together in hers. "No one is going to hurt you. That's the absolute last thing we'd want to do."

Megan stared at her, silent.

She could feel herself starting to relax, and her thoughts were beginning to slow down.

"I don't understand," Megan said. "What—"

"I'm going to explain everything," she said. "But first, I want to show you something."

Megan shook her head. "I don't want to see anything. Just tell me what's going on—"

Fiona held out her hand, and Megan looked down.

There was a small glass pyramid sitting in the middle of Fiona's palm. Megan had seen one before, the night they took Rachel. She tried to look away, but something wouldn't let her.

Deep inside the glass, she saw a steady blue pulse.

Growing brighter.

And then there was nothing.

33

*S*he feels small hands on her cheeks, and when she opens her eyes, she's on her back in a gray room.

No windows, no doors.

The child is kneeling over her, touching her face. She's saying something, repeating the same words again and again, but Megan can't hear.

She's focused on the girl's eyes, a deep, vivid blue.

Megan wants to reach out, to touch her, but she's afraid if she does, she'll disappear.

Instead, she says, "Hello."

The girl smiles at her.

Joy.

Megan feels it in her chest.

She starts to say more, but then the girl leans over her, close, her breath a whisper against Megan's skin.

"Wake up."

———

When Megan opened her eyes, she was sitting on a soft white couch in a pale-blue room. There was a bamboo coffee table in front of her and a large mirror mounted on the far wall. To her right were two wooden bookshelves with a door between them, and to her left, a row of floor-to-ceiling windows stretching the length of the room. Behind the glass, she saw only blue skies and white clouds.

She was wearing a hospital gown, and she was alone.

Megan stayed on the couch, staring out the windows, watching soft white clouds drift slowly by from left to right.

Time passed.

Then there was a knock at the door, and the latch clicked open. Megan turned toward the sound and watched as Fiona entered the room. She had on a long white coat, and she was carrying two small blue-and-white teacups.

"I thought you might like tea," she said, closing the door behind her. "Green, right?"

Fiona sat next to her on the couch and held out one of the cups. Megan stared at it for a moment before reaching out, slowly, and taking it.

The tea inside was pale green and cold.

"They're almost ready for you," Fiona said. "But I thought we could visit for a while first." She set her cup on the coffee table. "How are you feeling?"

Megan stared at the tea in her cup, silent.

Fiona reached out and touched her arm.

Megan looked up at her.

"How are you feeling, honey?"

Megan glanced back at the cup, then held it out to Fiona. She took it and set it on the table next to hers.

"Where are we?"

"This is my house," Fiona said. "Where I live."

"Your house?"

"Not the one by you," she said. "That's more of an office. This is where I live, at the Institute."

Megan's thoughts kept slipping away from her, and she frowned. "What's wrong with me?"

"You're being sedated," Fiona said. "We've found that it helps. It's nothing to worry about."

"Sedated?"

"The blue light." She motioned around the room. "Nanotechnology. The light sends our instructions along retinal pathways, allowing us to communicate with implanted nanites in your system. Those nanites target neurons in the VLPO of your hypothalamus. It's nothing to worry about."

Megan stared at her.

Fiona smiled. "The light makes you sleepy."

"Oh," Megan said. "Okay."

"Would you like to see the view?" Fiona asked. "I think you'll like it."

They stood, and Fiona led her to the windows. As they stepped close, Megan saw Willow Ridge unfurl beneath them, stretching out all the way to the horizon. It made her think of Tyler, and how he'd been right when he'd said the neighborhood looked fake from on top of the ridge.

Tyler.

"There's where you live." Fiona pointed down toward the left. "Fifth row in, and about halfway up, right in the middle of my section."

"Your section?"

"Five square blocks," she said. "It's my job to monitor all the units in that area, and that includes you."

"Where's Tyler?"

Fiona turned to her. "He's actually in the next building as we speak. He's doing well."

"Can I see him?"

"Not quite yet."

"Because of the experiment?"

Fiona sighed and shook her head. "I really dislike that term. *Experiment* makes what we do sound so nefarious, and nothing could be further from the truth. I much prefer the term *research and reintegration.*"

"But Mercer said—"

"David Mercer was confused." Fiona took her arm and led her back to the couch. "There's no experiment, Megan. All we're doing is developing a service, a life insurance policy if you will, that we hope to one day present to the public. We believe the demand for technology like ours will be overwhelming, but we'll let the market decide."

"I don't understand. What is this place?"

"This is a level-one reintegration facility," Fiona said.

"After a client expires, they are processed here at the Institute. Then they're assigned to a section in Willow Ridge where they can be monitored in a safe and controlled environment. A few long-term employees who have agreed to take part in the program are allowed limited contact with family members, and we encourage everyone to interact with the community in Ashland."

"The renovation project."

"That's right. Very good." She squeezed Megan's arm, gently. "The people in Ashland haven't always been as welcoming as we'd have liked, but we feel it's important for our clients to interact with a diverse group of people in a social setting before they're transferred to a less isolated, level-two site and made aware."

"Aware of what?"

"Of their new life." Fiona reached down and picked up Megan's teacup and handed it to her. "We delete all the memories associated with our client's death during processing, so when they regain consciousness, they're completely unaware of what has happened. In most cases, the hybrid transition is seamless, but we've found that if given time to acclimate in a safe, controlled environment, the psychological success rate during second-stage awareness is much higher."

"Hybrid?"

"Hybrid bionics," she said. "We restore function to the client's brain and nervous system, and we integrate an artificially intelligent interface capable of communicating with new DNA-specific organs transplanted into the body. We use nanotechnology to restore and repair damage from illness, injury, even from the aging process."

"Robots?"

Fiona laughed. "In a way, I suppose so. Although the body itself is organic, so no wires or circuits."

Megan watched as Fiona leaned forward, still laughing to herself, and picked up her teacup. She took a sip, frowned, and set the teacup down again.

"Mercer told me he remembered."

Fiona nodded. "Memories and emotions can resurface, but it's rare. In David Mercer's case, due to the unusual way he expired, his emotional response hasn't been ideal. We've had very little opportunity to work firsthand with suicides, for obvious reasons."

"The scars." Megan held her arms out, palms up, fighting to remember. "He tried to—"

"We've since altered our policy when it comes to unnatural deaths, but his case was early. There was no nullification clause in the event of a suicide, and his wife, Anna, was insistent. As a founder, her pull at the Institute was substantial. Although, the unpleasantness of Mercer's experience influenced her decision to forgo the procedure herself." Fiona paused. "Mercer has been a most challenging patient. I don't believe he'll ever be fully reintegrated."

Megan listened, trying to hold on to what Fiona was saying, but the meaning of the words drifted away from her, dissolving in her mind like smoke.

"Me?" she asked. "Tyler?"

"Your progress was delayed by the incident with Rachel, which was also a unique situation." Fiona leaned back into the corner of the couch and crossed her legs. "Because it took us longer than normal to recognize the problem with Mrs. Addison, you had time to come to your own conclusions. For you, awareness wasn't emotional, it was logical, and you were impressively persistent."

"Then I'm—"

"A client? Yes, both you and your husband."

Megan felt the teacup slip out of her hand. She heard the dull clink it made when it landed on the carpet at her feet, but she didn't realize what had happened until Fiona reached down to pick it up.

"Don't worry," Fiona said. "Easy to clean."

Megan glanced up at the blue light that seemed to leak into the room from every surface. Then she looked over at Fiona and said, "How?"

"Tyler's employee contract," she said. "You both signed on to his life insurance policy. The payout was much larger in return for agreeing to donate your bodies to the Institute for research."

"No," Megan said. "How did we—"

"Oh . . ." Fiona hesitated, shook her head. "I'm afraid that's not something we're allowed to discuss with—"

"Please?"

Fiona seemed to think about it for a moment. Then she set Megan's teacup on the coffee table and took her hands.

"You should know that after the procedure today, you won't remember this conversation. Your memories will be purged, so anything I tell you now is temporary."

"What happened?"

"There was a car accident," Fiona said. "It happened on the Fourth of July. According to the report, you were driving home from a party, and someone ran a red light. You and Tyler were processed immediately that night. Unfortunately, there was nothing we could do for Julia."

"Julia?"

Fiona nodded. "Children's brains aren't fully developed, so it isn't possible to integrate them with our technology. They're just not compatible."

Megan opened her mouth to ask, but then the lights in the room faded out and then back on again.

"That's us." Fiona stood and held out a hand to Megan. "Are we ready?"

Megan stared at her waiting hand, trying to hold on to the question in her mind, but it was already slipping away.

"It's okay," Fiona said. "There's nothing to worry about."

Megan nodded and took her hand.

34

F iona led Megan down a blue hallway toward a set of double doors. She pushed them open, and they stepped out into a bright courtyard filled with trees and grass and flowers, and surrounded on all sides by glass buildings that shone like crystal in the watery sunlight.

Megan stopped walking and looked around.

Then she felt Fiona's hand on her arm, leading her gently toward a winding brick path that cut across the courtyard toward another set of double doors.

"This way."

Megan followed her.

Fiona opened the doors and walked her down a long hallway and into a wide blue room. There was a circle of single beds arranged like flower petals around a large white pillar that ran from the floor to ceiling. On the surface of the pillar, above each bed, was a single black display rolling through a cascade of white numbers.

Megan stopped inside the doorway, stepped back.

"It's okay," Fiona said. "Don't be scared."

A woman in a white lab coat approached them and handed Fiona a clipboard. Fiona looked at the top page, flipped to the next, and said, "Nineteen is fine."

The woman nodded, took the clipboard, and crossed the room toward the pillar.

Fiona motioned for Megan to follow.

She didn't want to, but she did.

There were patients in a few of the beds, covered in pale-blue sheets and staring up at individual blue lights hovering over them. The tops of the lights were silver and connected to the beds by a long metal arm.

Several men and women in white lab coats and others in blue scrubs moved through the room, checking the displays and making notes on clipboards.

Megan looked down at an unconscious woman lying in one of the beds and saw a twist of translucent tubes running up from the floor and disappearing under the sheet.

"Where's Tyler?" Megan asked.

"Recovery," Fiona said. "But don't worry, he's doing fine. You'll see him before you know it."

"Okay."

She followed her around to the far side of the pillar. Fiona stopped at an empty bed and patted the thin mattress with her hand and said, "Hop on up."

Megan didn't move.

"Megan?"

She shook her head, stepped back.

Fiona moved closer. "If it makes you feel better, you're not going to be alone. I'll be here the entire time."

"I want to see Tyler."

"You will," Fiona said. "Just as soon as we're done here, I promise."

Megan didn't move.

The woman in the white lab coat who'd met them at the door approached with two men in blue scrubs. Fiona raised a hand, and they stopped a few feet away from the bed.

"Megan," Fiona said. "Look who else is here."

She stepped aside, motioning to the bed behind her.

David Mercer was lying on his back, staring up at the light above him. His face looked peaceful, his eyes wide and blue. The cluster of translucent tubes running under the sheets pulsed with a soft white light.

"See," Fiona said. "There's no reason to be scared."

Seeing Mercer made her chest ache, and she looked away. She knew that he was there because of her, that it was her fault, but the more she thought about it, the more her mind seemed to drift until there was nothing left.

"It's a very simple procedure," Fiona said. "And one you've been through before. I promise you won't remember any of it."

"Like Rachel?"

"That's right. Exactly like Rachel."

"And I can see Tyler?"

"Just as soon as we're done." Fiona patted the bed again. "Come on, honey. It'll be over before you know it."

Megan glanced back at the woman in the white lab coat and the two men in blue standing behind her. They were waiting, their eyes cold and unwavering.

Megan thought about seeing Tyler again, and that was enough to get her moving.

She stepped forward and sat on the bed.

"Go ahead and swing your feet up."

She did, and the woman in the white lab coat moved closer. Megan's hospital gown had slipped up around her knees, and the woman pulled it down. Then she reached for a sheet and covered her up to her neck before walking off toward the pillar.

Fiona leaned over her. She reached out and brushed the hair away from Megan's face. "Comfortable?"

Megan looked up at her. "Why do I have to forget?"

"It's standard procedure," she said. "We've found that anytime a first-stage patient experiences trauma, whether physical or mental, the chances of a successful integration drop dramatically, and we run an increased risk of rejection. Better to be safe."

Megan understood the words, but the meaning wasn't clear. She had more questions, but each time one came to her, it slipped easily from her mind, lost in the blue.

"We don't want you to have to worry about anything until you're ready," Fiona said. "All we want now is for you to be happy and safe and calm."

Megan felt tears snake down her cheeks. She thought she should reach up and wipe them away, but her arms were too heavy and she found she couldn't move.

Fiona noticed and frowned. "Why are you crying?"

"Because I don't want to forget."

"I'm sorry, honey, but it's the only way."

The tears kept coming, and Fiona stared at her for a moment. Then something changed in her eyes, and she put a hand on Megan's shoulder.

"You know what, hold on a minute."

Fiona motioned to the woman in the white coat. She met her at the foot of the bed, and Fiona walked her a few feet away to where Megan couldn't hear.

The woman listened as Fiona spoke, making notes on her clipboard. When Fiona finished talking, the woman showed her what she'd written. Fiona glanced at the clipboard, nodded, and the woman walked back toward the display above Megan's bed.

Then Fiona was back.

"Okay," she said. "It's all set."

"What is?"

"Because you're my favorite, I've arranged something special for you." She glanced down at her. "Do you know why you're my favorite?"

Megan didn't answer.

"Because you're different," she said. "You're rare, Megan, like finding a white buffalo. It's why we're all so excited about your progress. You represent a huge step forward for the program."

"I don't understand."

"True individuality." Fiona put a hand on Megan's arm. "In most patients there's a personality shift. They slip easily into their roles at Willow Ridge, and they lose that spark that made them unique. But not you. From the very beginning you wanted something more, and you showed true independent thought. That makes you—"

"Your favorite."

"Exactly," Fiona said. "And that's why I've arranged something special for you. Consider it a gift. You won't remember it when we're through, but I think you'll enjoy it while it lasts."

"What kind of gift?"

"I'm going to show you something beautiful," she said. "Something precious."

Behind her, Megan heard the low mechanical whirl of the machine inside the pillar. She wanted to see, but Fiona was next to her, and Megan couldn't look away.

"I don't understand."

"I know," Fiona said. "But you will."

The woman in the white lab coat came back. She had a coil of translucent tubes in her hand. At the end of each tube was a long silver needle.

The woman nodded to Fiona.

"Okay," Fiona said. "Here we go."

She bent and pressed a button on the side of the bed, and Megan heard a hydraulic hiss behind her head. Then, slowly, a silver disk moved into sight over her. There were several dead black spots on the surface, and between them, her reflection.

"What is this?"

Fiona adjusted the silver disk above her and said, "This is just the beginning, honey."

Megan wanted to ask more; she wanted to know how long it would take and what kind of gift Fiona was giving her. But before she could find the words, the dead spots on the silver surface shone a familiar ice blue, and Megan felt her entire body contract, and her thoughts slip away.

Then, before the world flashed blue, she heard a small voice, soft and lovely.

One word, barely a whisper.

"*Mommy . . .*"

35

*W*ake up."
Megan opens her eyes and she's home, in her apartment in Chicago. Julia is next to her, pulling herself up onto the bed. Then she's on her knees, leaning over her, small hands touching Megan's face, dark hair tickling her skin.

Julia's blue eyes . . .

"Mommy," she whispers. "Wake up."

Megan reaches out and gently moves the hair from her face. Then she pulls her close and kisses her forehead.

"Okay," she says. "I'm awake."

Tyler stirs next to them, and Julia climbs over, landing on top of him, elbows and knees. He makes a breathless sound, then tickles her and lifts her up, squealing, into the air.

"What is this? Who are you?"

Julia laughs, trying to catch her breath.

"Daddy!"

Megan smiles, pushes the sheets back, and swings her legs out of bed. She walks out into the hallway toward the bathroom, hearing the buzz of the city outside and Julia's laughter behind her.

When she gets to the bathroom, she stops and looks back down the hallway toward Tyler and Julia. For an instant, her bedroom is gone and all she sees through the doorway is a blue room and a woman in a long white lab coat standing at the far end, watching her.

Megan closes her eyes.

When she looks again, she sees the redbrick walls of her bedroom and Julia running out, giggling, her white nightgown billowing around bruised knees. Tyler is standing on the other side of the bed, shirtless, with his back to her. He reaches over his head, stretches, then pulls the curtains back from the window.

The sun shines in, bright and blinding.

Megan loses herself in the light.

———

And the world flashed blue.

———

The line moves, and they step up to the counter. The girl working the register smiles, and Megan says, "Two strawberry and one lime, please."

The girl scrapes shaved ice into paper cones and soaks them in neon red and green. She hands them to Megan across the counter while Tyler pays. To her left, a woman standing at the ring toss game laughs as the man working the booth hands her a giant stuffed rabbit. While to her right, the carousel turns, the calliope music swells, and the amber lights crowning the top of the ride glow and spin in the early evening air.

Megan stops walking.

"Something wrong?" Tyler slips an arm around her shoulders and bites his red snow cone. "You look lost."

"It's nothing," she says. "Déjà vu."

Tyler nods, takes another bite. Some of the ice falls, hitting his white shirt, leaving a blood-red spot on his chest.

Megan sees it, and something deep inside of her wants to scream.

Then Julia runs up, grabs her hand.

"Come on, you promised."

Megan glances down at her. "It's getting late. If we don't go soon, we'll miss the fireworks."

"You two go ahead," Tyler says. "I'll get the car and pull around by the gate. We'll make it in time."

Julia cheers and pulls Megan away.

She waves to Tyler and follows Julia through the maze of booths and people, light and shadow, toward the Ferris wheel turning slowly in the blue distance.

They make it just in time.

They climb on, and the wheel spins, carrying them up. When it stops at the top, Julia moves closer and squeezes Megan's arm tight.

"Are you scared?" Megan asks.

"No," she says. "I'm not scared."

Megan smiles to herself, then puts her arm around Julia's shoulder and pulls her in.

"Of course you're not."

She looks out over the edge at the carnival below, then up, over the trees, toward the skyline of the city just starting to glitter against the fading daylight.

"It's pretty, isn't it?"

Julia nods, trembles against her.

Megan looks down at her, and for an instant, she remembers the child as a baby–how she would fall asleep in her arms, her head resting against her shoulder, her warm breath soft on her neck.

Megan kisses Julia's head, holds her tighter.

———

And the world flashed blue.

———

"You made it."

The woman who answers the door has a glass of red wine in her hand, and she leans forward and hugs them both. Then she looks down at Julia, smiles, places a hand on her head.

"Everyone is on the roof with the drinks," she says. "I was on my way up, too."

"Have the fireworks started?" Julia asks.

"Not yet," the woman says. "They're late this year."

Julia smiles, bounces.

"Go on up," the woman says. "I'm right behind you."

"Anything we can help with?" Tyler asks.

"No, you go ahead," she says. "Grab a drink. There's beer in the cooler and wine on the bar. I'm getting more ice, but I'm right behind you."

Julia turns and runs down the hall toward the metal door leading to the stairs.

Tyler yells after her, telling her to wait. Then he looks back and shrugs. "I'll see you two up there."

Megan watches him go, then turns back to the woman and says, "Let me help you."

"There's only two bags," she says. "We can each take one. Grab a glass of wine. There's a bottle on the counter and glasses in the cabinet."

"Thanks," Megan says. "But I'm not drinking."

The woman laughs. "That's something I don't hear very of-

ten." She starts to say more, but then the look on her face changes and she stops, stares at her.

Megan tries not to smile.

"You're fucking kidding me?"

"Tyler doesn't know," Megan says. "I was going to tell him tonight."

The woman sets her glass down and wraps her arms around Megan's neck, pulling her in. "Oh my God. This is the best news. I'm so happy for you."

"You can't let on that you know."

"Are you kidding?" The woman steps back, looks down at Megan's stomach, then up at her eyes. "This is perfect and it's meant to be. You've come so far, and now this."

"I just wish Mom were here to—"

"Don't do that." The woman puts her hands on Megan's shoulders, squeezes. "This is a happy time, kiddo. Mom wouldn't want you to be sad."

Megan nods, tries to smile.

The woman smiles back, wipes away tears. "Holy shit, I'm going to be an aunt."

"You're already an aunt."

"Yeah, I know," she says. "But it never gets old."

They carry the ice to the roof, talking and laughing along the way. When they step out into the night, Megan sees Tyler and Julia on the other side by the ledge. He's on one knee, beer in hand, pointing out toward the sky.

Megan starts toward them, looking out, trying to see what they see, but all she sees is a dim charcoal haze.

"What are you two looking at?"

Julia turns around, smiles, and points to a small blue dot hovering over the horizon. "Neptune," she says. "It's the blue planet because it's covered in water."

Megan frowns and looks at Tyler.

"Why do you tell her these things?"

He winks and takes a drink. "Come on, let's find a seat. The fireworks are about to start."

They move back toward the crowd. There are lawn chairs set up all along the roof. Megan sits in a pale-green chair and Julia climbs on her lap.

"There's no water on Neptune?"

"Afraid not."

Julia looks at her skeptically. "Then why's it blue?"

Megan thinks back, trying to remember what her father had told her when she was young, back when they'd spend their summers camping, their nights sitting around a fire, talking, telling stories, and staring at the stars.

"It has something to do with its atmosphere," Megan says. "It's made up of different gases, and when the sun shines on them, those gases absorb the light, but they reflect the color blue back into space."

"Why?"

"It's just the way it is."

Julia seems to think about this. Then she leans back against her and says, "Blue is my favorite color."

"Mine too."

When the fireworks start, Julia stays on her lap, and by the time they end, she's asleep.

Next to her, Megan watches Tyler reach into the cooler and take out a beer. He opens it, then digs into his pocket and takes out his car keys.

He hands them to her.

"How many have you had?" she asks.

"Enough to know better. Are you okay driving tonight?"

She tells him she is, and for a moment she just sits there, looking up at him, this man, his keys in her hand, and their daughter asleep on her lap.

"What?" he asks. "Something wrong?"

"No," she says. "Nothing's wrong."

"Then why are you looking at me like that?"

Megan pauses. "Do you really want to know?"

"Desperately."

She laughs and motions him closer.

Tyler turns in his chair and inches forward, smiling.

Megan sits up. Then she turns and glances out at the sky and the tiny blue dot sitting just above the horizon.

Tyler waits. "Well?"

Megan looks over at him, leans in.

As she gets close, she can smell the comforting sweetness of his skin, and she can feel the warmth of his cheek against hers. She stays like that for as long as she can, trying to memorize every detail of the moment.

Then, when she's sure she'll never forget, she moves her lips close to his ear and whispers . . .

———

And the world flashed blue.

36

T hen it was Saturday morning.

Megan awoke to sunlight and the smell of fresh coffee. She could hear the shower running in the bathroom, and she sat up, fast, her heart beating hard inside her chest. She looked over at Tyler's side of the bed, saw the wrinkled sheets, and a calming wave of relief washed over her.

Bad dream?

She eased back down, lying on her side, and touched the spot where he'd slept the night before. She couldn't quite recall what the dream had been about, and the harder she tried, the more the images faded.

Megan stayed in bed for a while, listening to the blue jays argue beneath her window. Then she pushed the sheets away and stood up.

Her robe was hanging on the back of the door, and she slipped it on as she walked into the hallway and down the stairs toward the kitchen. She could hear the slow tick of the grandfather clock as she passed the living room, but she was still thinking about the bad dream from the night before and barely noticed the sound.

She stepped into the kitchen.

The light coming in through the window was bright, and the room felt clean and warm. Her yellow coffee cup was sitting upside down in the dish drainer, and she took it out and set it on the counter.

She reached for the coffeepot and poured.

Upstairs, the shower shut off.

She smiled, replaced the pot, and carried the cup into the living room. As she passed the couch, she noticed a new book sitting on the coffee table.

She stopped to pick it up.

On the cover was a large black rabbit, silhouetted in front of a burnt-orange sun.

Megan frowned. She set her cup on the table and turned the book over, scanning the back. It wasn't hers, and she assumed Tyler had bought it for her to read.

The thought warmed her.

She sat on the couch and flipped through the pages. The book opened naturally to a spot in the middle, as if something had been pressed inside, and she saw that one of the lines on the page had been underlined in blue ink.

Megan read it and frowned.

My heart has joined the thousand.

Something about the line was familiar, even though she didn't think she'd read the book. At least, she thought she hadn't. It was possible she'd read it a long time ago and had forgotten, which was fine. She was always looking for something new to read, and the book looked interesting, even if it was about rabbits.

Megan closed the book and set it back on the coffee table. Then she got up, grabbed her coffee cup, and carried it to the window and looked out over the neighborhood.

The sun was shining, and the sky was clear and blue. The cypress trees in the yards stood tall and thin, and the lilac bushes running between the houses swayed softly in the gentle morning breeze.

Next door, Edna Davidson was outside talking to a young couple with a black Lab on the end of a brown leather leash. She had Mr. Jitters cradled in her arms, and he kept looking down at the other dog, trembling and terrified.

The black Lab didn't seem to notice him at all.

Across the street, a woman in a white button-up shirt and faded jeans was walking along the sidewalk, moving from house to house, ringing doorbells. She had a wooden clipboard in her hand, and she made notes as she went.

Megan sipped her coffee and glanced down at the corner house across the street. As always, Rachel Addison, in her floppy white sun hat and oversized sunglasses, was outside with her pruning shears. She was kneeling in front of a rainbow of roses, each one vibrating in the sunlight.

Megan watched her for a long time, wondering how she managed to grow such beautiful flowers.

Someday, she thought, she'd discover her secret.

Her cup was almost empty, and she was about to go back to the kitchen for a refill when the doorbell rang.

She finished the last of the coffee in one swallow, then went to answer the door.

The woman she'd seen earlier, walking from house to house with the clipboard, was standing on her porch, smiling at her.

Megan smiled back.

"Hi." The woman squeezed the clipboard against her chest and held out her hand. "I'm Fiona Matheson. I live a few blocks down."

"Megan Stokes."

They shook, and Fiona held Megan's hand as she spoke.

"I hope this isn't a bad time," she said. "I've been meaning to come by and introduce myself for a while. I try to meet all the new neighbors. I'm usually pretty good about it, but lately it's just been one thing after another."

Megan smiled, didn't speak.

"Anyway, I was in the area, and when I saw your house, I thought I'd stop by and say hello."

"That's nice, thank you."

"How are you guys adjusting to Stepford?"

"Stepford?"

Fiona laughed and waved the comment away. "It's an old joke around here, but it fits, don't you think?"

Megan tried to smile. "Oh, I don't know. Not really."

The light behind Fiona's eyes seemed to dim slightly, like watching a cloud pass in front of the sun.

"Well, like I said. It's an old joke."

Megan nodded, and for a moment they were both quiet. Then Fiona motioned toward the street and said, "Listen, I don't want to keep you. I know it's early, and you probably have a busy day."

"Okay."

Fiona paused, then pulled a small white business card from the clipboard. She flipped it over and wrote on the back.

"This is me." She handed the card to Megan. "If you're not busy sometime, give me a call. I know moving to a new place can be tough, especially one like this."

"Thanks," Megan said. "I wasn't sure I'd like it here at first, but it's grown on me. I think it's nice."

Fiona smiled, but it didn't touch her eyes.

"In that case maybe we can have a glass of wine or two some night and talk. Get to know each other."

"Oh," Megan said. "I'm afraid I don't drink."

"You don't drink?"

Megan shook her head, and the silence hung heavy between them. When Fiona spoke next, her voice was flat.

"Well, keep my number anyway, you never know."

Megan thanked her and closed the door.

She pocketed the card in her robe, then went into the kitchen and refilled her coffee cup. She carried it back to the living room and stood at the window and looked out.

Time passed.

Then Tyler came into the room.

He had his blue tie draped loose around his neck, and he was carrying his travel mug in one hand while patting his pockets with the other.

"Have you seen my keys?" he asked. "I have no idea what I did with them."

Megan stared at him, and when the thought hit her, it hit hard.

They're in his pocket.

His keys are in his pocket.

"Megs, have you seen them? I'm going to be late."

It took her a second to shake the thought away and find her voice again. When she did, she pointed toward the door. "Did you check the bowl?"

Tyler hurried to the front door, and she heard the delicate clink of metal on metal. Then he turned, holding them up, his finger through the ring.

"Found them."

"Glad I could help."

Tyler crossed the room to where she was standing. He set his travel mug and the keys on the table, then wrapped his arms around her from behind and kissed her neck.

Megan made a soft sound and pressed against him. "I thought you said you were going to be late?"

"On a Saturday?" He kissed her again. "Who cares?"

She turned, set her coffee cup on the table, and put her hands on his cheeks and kissed him, long and slow.

When they broke, she stared at him and said, "I had the worst dream last night."

"What about?"

She shook her head. "I've been trying to remember, but it keeps slipping away."

"That's the best kind of bad dream to have."

"I guess so," she said, but she still stared at him for a moment longer, trying to remember. "It's just—"

"No." Tyler reached out and turned her around so she was facing the window. "No more bad dreams."

He put his hands on her waist and his chin on her shoulder and they both stood there, staring out at the green world and the blue sky.

"Who was at the door?"

"The Willow Ridge welcoming committee."

"Really?"

"No, not really. It was one of our neighbors stopping by to say hello and welcome us to Stepford."

Tyler frowned. "Stepford?"

"I think it was a joke."

He kissed her neck. "I don't get it."

Megan shrugged. "I guess it's an old one."

Outside, a vintage yellow car with a long white stripe running along the side drove by. An old man with a white beard sat smiling behind the wheel.

Tyler whistled. "Wow, look at that."

"Since when do you care about old cars?"

"I can appreciate them," he said. "And you don't see many like that around here. I wonder what it is."

"It's a 1957 Chevy Bel Air."

Tyler pulled back, staring at her. "How the hell do you know that?"

Megan had no idea how she knew, but the tone of his voice annoyed her, and she frowned.

"Why would you assume I wouldn't know?"

Tyler's eyes narrowed.

"And it's not an *it*, it's a *she*," Megan said. "Cars are always female."

This time, Tyler laughed.

"Of course they are."

Neither of them said anything for a while as they stood together at the window, watching the yellow car pass in front of the house. It stopped at the top of the street and turned right at the intersection, disappearing behind a wall of hedges.

"I should probably go," Tyler said. "I'll see you tonight, soon as I can."

Megan turned and reached out, grabbing the two loose ends of his tie, helping him make the knot. When she finished, she stood on her toes and angled up to kiss him.

His lips felt soft and warm on hers.

"I'll be here," she said.

After he left, she stood at the window and watched as he

pulled out of the driveway.

She waved to him.

He waved back.

And then he was gone.

She stayed at the window for a while longer, finishing the last of her coffee. Then she carried the empty cup back to the kitchen and rinsed it in the sink before shutting off the water and setting the cup upside down in the dish drainer.

Ready for a new day.

Megan shook the water from her hands and reached for the towel on the counter. Outside, she could hear the angry chatter of the blue jays, complaining in the sunlight.

The sound made her smile.

She wondered what, in such a beautiful world, could they possibly be so upset about.

ACKNOWLEDGMENTS

Thank you to my agent, Scott Miller, and to my editor, Gracie Doyle. Thank you to Jeff Belle, Mikyla Bruder, Hai-Yen Mura, Dennelle Catlett, Laura Costantino, Gabrielle Guarnero, Laura Barrett, Sarah Shaw, and everyone on the Thomas & Mercer team. Thank you to Caitlin Alexander for editing this book, and to my early readers, Kurt Dinan, Kimberly A. Bettes, Christina Frans, Mike McCrary, Kimberly Collison, Peter Farris, Marni Valerio, Grant Jerkins, and John Mantooth for their time and keen insight. I'd also like to thank my friends Keith Rawson, Sean Chercover, Jacque Ben-Zekry, and Blake Crouch who all, at one time or another, encouraged me to reach a little further with this story, and to trust my instincts. And finally, as always, I want to thank my wife, Amy, for once again making all of this possible.

ABOUT THE AUTHOR

John Rector is the bestselling author of the novels *The Cold Kiss, The Grove, Already Gone, Out of the Black,* and *Ruthless.* His short fiction has appeared in numerous magazines and has won several awards, including the International Thriller Award for his novella, *Lost Things.* He lives in Omaha, Nebraska.